"You will not be able to retain your position if you do not comply, Livia."

She looked up at him, at his face that had become so dear to her. At this palace that had been her home these many years.

"Then I quit."

She stood up from her desk and looked down at the planners there. They contained...everything. Every detail about what Matteo would be doing for the next year. Everything planned absolutely down to the minute. She had coordinated all of it.

And he wanted her to be his wife.

No. Just no.

For living and working with Matteo and knowing she could never have him was bad enough. Having him and still not having him would be even worse.

"You cannot quit."

She shrugged. "I have."

She would leave those planners. Leave them behind and never look back on them again. Never think about them again. Because all things considered, she would rather die than become Matteo's consolation wife.

"You cannot leave me," he said.

"I can," she said, feeling buoyant now. "I will. And I will not marry you, Matteo. Not for anything."

Millie Adams has always loved books. She considers herself a mix of Anne Shirley (loquacious but charming and willing to break a slate over a boy's head if need be) and Charlotte Doyle (a lady at heart, but with the spirit to become a mutineer should the occasion arise). Millie lives in a small house on the edge of the woods, which she finds allows her to escape in the way she loves best—in the pages of a book. She loves intense alpha heroes and the women who dare to go toe-to-toe with them (or break a slate over their heads).

Books by Millie Adams

Harlequin Presents

The Kings of California

The Scandal Behind the Italian's Wedding
Stealing the Promised Princess

Visit the Author Profile page
at Harlequin.com for more titles.

Millie Adams

CROWNING HIS INNOCENT ASSISTANT

HARLEQUIN

PRESENTS

Recycling programs
for this product may
not exist in your area.

ISBN-13: 978-1-335-40395-7

Crowning His Innocent Assistant

Copyright © 2021 by Millie Adams

All rights reserved. No part of this book may be used or reproduced in
any manner whatsoever without written permission except in the case of
brief quotations embodied in critical articles and reviews.

This is a work of fiction. Names, characters, places and incidents
are either the product of the author's imagination or are used fictitiously.
Any resemblance to actual persons, living or dead, businesses,
companies, events or locales is entirely coincidental.

This edition published by arrangement with Harlequin Books S.A.

For questions and comments about the quality of this book,
please contact us at CustomerService@Harlequin.com.

Harlequin Enterprises ULC
22 Adelaide St. West, 40th Floor
Toronto, Ontario M5H 4E3, Canada
www.Harlequin.com

Printed in U.S.A.

CROWNING HIS INNOCENT ASSISTANT

For those who feel small or timid. You have more strength in you than you know. Remember it was a mouse who pulled the thorn from the lion's paw, not with great shows of strength but with the courage of character.

CHAPTER ONE

MATTEO DE LA CRUZ, King of Monte Blanco, sovereign leader of all he surveyed, from the deep green trees to the white mountains in the distance, strode into his well-appointed office in the very highest tower of the Monte Blancan palace, where he found his assistant, just as he had expected to find her: sitting at her desk, tapping away on her laptop.

She had four paper planners laid out in front of her, and pens of different colors sitting on each one. She was neat and orderly, it was true, but when she worked, she kept all resources handily at her fingertips.

Livia.

No last name, as she had no family. She was simply Livia. Though, he often called her by the preferred nickname. Mouse. He didn't know if she preferred it, but when it came right down to it, it didn't matter.

He preferred it.

He did not, though, call her Mouse for the reasons his brother, Prince Javier, supposed. It was not because she was gray or small. Not because she was timid or plain. No, he called her that because as king, he was a lion.

And there were times when he felt as if she, with all her small delicacy, had removed a thorn from his paw when she had come into his life.

A stunning admission for a man such as himself to make, it was true. But if he were honest, and he was, bracingly so, he had been told many times, then he had to admit that he had most certainly changed Livia's life for the best as well. His mouse had been utterly and completely without resources when he had found her, a thin, pale guttersnipe who had been weighing in on the brink of starvation when he had discovered her.

It had been just after the death of his father, and he, the newly crowned king, had been taking in the sights of Monte Blanco, a country in much need of rehabilitation after being beneath the iron fist of a cruel dictator.

That was when he had seen her in the snow. Huddled in an alleyway and shivering.

He had picked her up and brought her into the limousine. And she had regarded him with wide, wary eyes. He couldn't blame her. It was clear that the world had not been kind to the shivering little thing he had brought inside his car.

But he had purposed, then and there, that he would be.

She was a symbol.

A symbol of the reform that he planned to bring to Monte Blanco. He had given her work at the palace, after giving her a place to sleep and making sure that she'd been given adequate food. But he had never found it... Well, she didn't have family. And he had not wanted to install her in the servants' quarters on the property. She had seemed too vulnerable to him at the time. Instead, he had given her a bedroom in the palace, which was highly unusual. He had noticed that she had an eye for organization, because he was very good at recognizing the talents of other people in implementing them to his greatest advantage. And that was when he had hit upon the idea of her being his assistant.

Over the years she had become a great deal more than that.

When his father had died, Matteo had expelled each and every advisor that had ever been in the old man's ear from ever setting foot in the palace again. He had started anew.

And so, Livia had become his assistant, his majordomo, his advisor, all rolled into one.

Livia was... Quite simply *his*. In every way.

His assistant.

His mouse.

And after today, very soon to be something else.

"Livia," he said, "I've been looking for you."

"I am exactly where I am always at this time

of day, Your Majesty, unless we are off at another scheduled engagement, which you know we are not."

"True," he said. "I have something to discuss with you."

"Go on," she said, without looking up from her computer.

Her delicate features were placid, a round pair of glasses perched on the end of her nose. Her light brown hair was piled atop her head, wispy strands escaping around her face. She had such fine little features. Very large eyes with pale spiky-tipped lashes hiding behind those glasses. A nose that pointed upward with decisiveness.

Her mouth was unique. Her upper lip larger than her lower, curving dramatically upward toward the center before sloping down at the edges, giving her a permanent pout. Her hands were delicate, finely honed, and efficient as they moved over the keys.

And if her strange sort of beauty had bewitched him at times over the years, he'd become good at ignoring it. For he was a king. And she was…

Her.

And he knew that the computer in front of her held less information than her mind. For she remembered every detail of every single thing. In fact, Matteo himself had to remember nothing because it all resided inside of Livia's brain.

He was a king, and as such had a great many important things that must be thought of at all times.

He had to remember how to keep the entire king-dom running.

He could not bother himself with details. Livia was the keeper of the details.

He kept the world spinning, she kept the day running. Between the two of them, it was quite perfect.

"Now that Violet and Javier have wed, I find my-self quite without a fiancée."

"That's true," she said, her eyes not so much as flicking up from the screen.

"And I have been thinking."

"Mm," she said, the noise vaguely disinterested.

"You should be my wife, Livia."

"No." Her face did not budge, her fingers did not pause in their keystrokes. She acted as if he had said nothing half so remarkable as giving her a report on the weather.

"No?"

"No," she reiterated.

"It was not a question."

"Traditionally," she said, her tone maddeningly patient, her focus still on the computer, "such things are phrased as questions. As it is helpful to have the other party's permission."

Matteo waved his hand. "I do not need permission."

"*Indeed.* All the same, no." She continued typing away.

"It makes sense," he countered.

"So does the rather popular candy combination

of chocolate and peanut butter, but I find it abhorrent nonetheless."

"I need a wife."

"And I can find you one. But I will not be your wife."

Men trembled in the wake of his disapproval. She did not so much as bat one spiked lash.

"Livia, surely you must acknowledge the great honor that I extend to you."

She did look up then, her enormous, violet eyes filled with disdain.

Disdain.

Not only had she outright refused him, an event he could not remember experiencing ever before in his life, she now disdained him. His mouse. The woman he had lifted from a gutter. He was offering her a chance to become Queen.

Queen.

To rise above the position of secretary, and she'd said no.

"I do not wish your honor. If it is such a great boon, extend it to someone else and they will no doubt be thrilled. For I will not reach out and grab *that* particular royal scepter. As flattering as it is to be offered the position after you have been denied by someone else, as wonderful as it surely is to be given a hand-me-down title rejected by another, I would think that you were much better off handling this the way most royals do."

"And how is that?"

"Well, I'm not royal, am I? So I'm not entirely sure. Political intrigue? A magical ball where all the young ladies of the land are invited to show off their wares? Inviting them to spend the night atop the heap of twenty mattresses and seeing who can feel the pea at the bottom. I don't know."

Matteo had a will of iron and he'd yet to find anyone who could meaningfully test it. Somehow, she was. "You do not have the right to refuse me."

"Will you throw me in the dungeon?" She stared him down blinking slowly and she did indeed put him in the mind of a mouse, but not as many people might imagine one of the small rodents. No. For she was not skittish and easily spooked. She was bright-eyed and immovable. And he had the feeling that if he made the wrong move, she would slip through his grasp completely.

"You don't think I will?"

"No, I don't. Because you and I both know that you're not the sort of king who leaves people to rot in dungeons, are you? That was your father. And you're not your father. You do a very good impersonation of an arrogant ass, but you're not a cruel man, and we both know it."

"I could've left you by the side of the road."

"You couldn't have. Your great tragedy, Matteo, is that you have a heart. Encrusted in coal though it may be."

"Livia, I have thought this over extensively. I am

a man who knows his duty to his country, to his people. I'm a man who understands the office of Queen, and what will be required of her. And I have decided that you are the one to fill that office."

"You are mistaken, with respect, Your Majesty."

"Mouse…"

Her gaze sharpened. "I'm not a seventeen-year-old girl. Not anymore. I cannot be swayed by the fear of losing all that you've given me. Nor will I be swayed by the fear of losing the great blessing of being in your presence. You cannot threaten me. You cannot manipulate me."

She looked back at her computer screen. And Matteo was confronted by the fact that he might very well have met an object he could not move.

Livia wished, very much, that she could say she was surprised by Matteo's proposal. But no. In fact, by her calculations he was almost a full day early in his proposal from her original estimation, which was maybe the only surprising part about it.

She had known it was coming.

She had known it with a strange, depressing sort of certainty that really didn't bear mulling over much. She had been counting on this, from the moment that she had found out his marriage to Violet King was off because she had taken up with his brother, Prince Javier.

Yes, she had known that Matteo's proposal would be coming.

The worst part was, when Matteo's engagement to Violet had been dissolved, she'd experienced a moment of absolute and complete joy. She had let the rush of all her girlish fantasies come back and flood her, fill her with the kind of hope that women with her background simply couldn't afford to have.

But she had allowed it for a moment.

Just for a moment.

She had allowed herself to wonder. *What if.* To dream. It was so easy for her to conjure up the image of her perfect wedding. A royal one, large and lavish— not so much because it was what she wanted, but because it came with loving a king.

And she did love him. She had from the time she'd been a seventeen-year-old girl plucked out of the gutter by his royal hand. How could she not?

He was the most devastatingly handsome man she had ever seen. Of course, she'd been terrified of him at first, for he was not a safe sort of beast. No. He was a lion. Regal and majestic, and utterly capable of devastating any foe that came his way; willing and able to flex his unparalleled strength if need be. It had been obvious to her from the beginning, no matter that he tried to affect the posture of a civilized man, that Matteo was anything but. He had made a concerted effort to show the people of Monte Blanco that he was not his father. That his rule would not be marked by the same scorch that his father's reign had. There would be no dungeons. There would be no imprisonments. No more people disappearing in the dead of night for an imagined whisper against the King. No. There would be none of that. He had promised it would be so.

But she had known, always, that the same sort of danger lurked beneath the surface of Matteo's skin. And she didn't think it was simply because she had spent years out on the streets avoiding the dangers all around her.

Not *only* that, at least.

But in spite of the danger he represented, or perhaps because of it, she had found herself becoming utterly infatuated with him.

And she had known there was no way the two of them could ever be together.

She was an urchin. And a rather plain one at that.

And he was… He was the King.

At least, that was what she had thought then, with all her silly, girlish hopes. But over the years, she could see that Matteo had started to think of her as a sort of Swiss Army knife; a woman who could, and did, perform any task he so desired. And as a result, she had realized—after the high of her joy over his broken engagement had worn off—that there was no chance at all he wasn't going to seize the opportunity to have a Swiss Army wife. It was just the sort of man he was.

And she knew that had nothing to do with the way he felt about her, not personally. It had everything to do with how she could serve him. And the idea of being in a perfunctory, passionless marriage with Matteo honestly made her wish she was dead.

Because she had spent years living beneath his notice. Years sending breakup gifts to the various mistresses that he had cast off. Coming up with excuses for why he couldn't meet them, and in general, dealing with discreet rendezvous. She had seen the women he liked. Even Violet King, Javier's wife and Matteo's former fiancée, hadn't been quite his type of beauty.

She had a modern sensibility about her. Curvy and vivacious, and incredibly beautiful as far as Livia was concerned. But the women that Matteo preferred were icy, statuesque. Women who matched up to his imposing frame. Who had the same sort of sophistication that he carried with him.

Yes, those were the women that Matteo loved. *Socialites*.

Human icicles with platinum hair, wrapped in couture. Livia, for her part, barely came to the middle of his chest. When she wore heels, she could acquaint herself better with the bottom of his chin. She did not possess the sort of vapid wit that seemed to come as a standard feature on those particular models of women. Smiles that would cut with the accuracy of a knife while externally appearing to be the advertisement for a gum commercial. Saccharine and white and altogether pristine.

None of the women were airheads, of course, for if they had been Matteo would not have been able to bear them. But they all did a strange sort of half-giggle, before sharpening their words into spears and aiming them at the unsuspecting targets who truly did think that blondes had more fun and less brain cells.

They were to be commended in that way, Livia hated to admit. For they were women who had managed to take both the advantages and disadvantages given to them by society and turn them into something useful.

Livia had two assets. Two very real assets. The first was that she was stubborn. Utterly and completely. It was that stubbornness that helped her deal with heads of state who were trying to elbow their way into Matteo's schedule. With ex-girlfriends who wanted an audience with a man that Livia knew didn't want one with them; with party planners and media personnel; and with any other number of people who had to pass through her in an attempt to get to Matteo.

The second was that she forgot *nothing*. And so, could remember without fail whether Matteo had actually said he was waiting for a particular person's call, or suss out if they were lying. She could remember if he had ended things with a particular blonde model or not. If there was credibility to her claim she could be bearing his child based on timing… Yes, she was the keeper of all manner of trivial knowledge and an excessive amount of stubbornness. But none of those things made her think that Matteo had suddenly grown an intense attraction to her. No. But why did he have to be *quite so predictable*?

She would have been pleased if he would've come in and asked her to help arrange a ball. It was that she did know him quite so well, that she was this right about him, that distressed her. Because she knew what he liked, and it wasn't her. And she had also known that he would go for convenience before he went for anything else.

"You will not be able to retain your position if you do not comply, Livia."

She looked up at him, at his face that had become so dear to her. At this palace that had been her home these many years. Matteo paid her well. Generously. She did not stay on because she had to. She had also learned any number of valuable skills while in his employ. She had compiled education enough to have several degrees and had vast experience as an assistant. She was discreet and had worked with the highest level of state in Monte Blanco. Yes, she did not fear for her future should she choose to leave. It wasn't what had kept her here. But this was the end point, she could see it now.

"Then I quit."

She stood up from her desk and looked down at the

planners there. They contained…everything. Every detail about what Matteo would be doing for the next year. Everything planned absolutely down to the minute. Along with what he would wear, whom he would speak to, where cars would pick him up from.

She had coordinated all of it.

Where his private plane would fly, where it would refuel, which places he might pass through to make the most of the political opportunity. Even what she would wear. For she was always on hand at public events. She always wore black. Always blended into the background. She treated herself like a member of serving staff. Hanging at the outside, in case he ever needed her. Unremarkable. Unnoticed. *His mouse.* A small dowdy creature who might as well live in the walls of the palace for all that he noticed her when he didn't need something.

And he wanted her to be his wife.

No. Just no.

For living with, and working with, Matteo knowing she could never have him was bad enough. Having him and still not having him would be even worse.

"You cannot quit."

She shrugged. "I have."

She would leave those planners. Leave them behind and never look back on them again. Never think about them again. The sudden surge of joy that brought her was indescribable. The only thing that it matched was the moment she had found out that Matteo was no longer going to marry Violet. And she had a feeling that it would be matched by a similar crash when the reality of everything hit her, but for now she felt... New. Empowered. She would not marry him. And she would not be his assistant anymore. Maybe she wouldn't even stay in Monte Blanco.

That determination had been beyond the girl she had been when he had picked her up on the side of the road. That girl, that creature, hadn't been able to choose or decide anything. She had been cold and angry and bitter. She had a knife in her boot for the express purpose of stabbing men who had tried to take liberties with her. And she had used it.

And the men had not succeeded.

Starvation had made her mean. And when she had found morsels of food, she hadn't wanted to share them with anyone. Not even the visibly hungry people she shared the streets with.

That girl had not been able to imagine anything beyond the next sunrise. She had not been able to imagine anything that wasn't hunger, sadness or desolation.

She had not been able to imagine a future where she had become the personal assistant to the King. And then feel empowered enough in her own self to walk away from that same King, rather than accepting his offer of becoming Queen.

She wished she could go back and tell that Livia. The one that had been on the streets for years after being dumped there by her mother.

Unwanted.

With ease, she could remember the pain, the fear, that she had felt when she had stood alone in that busy carnival, holding a bunch of cotton candy and looking around, sure that her mother must be around somewhere. Sure that she would come back for her. It had taken days for her to accept that her mother had well and truly left her.

On purpose.

In a carnival with a last treat like it might mask the pain of having been abandoned. It hadn't. Nothing could. Nothing did. She had been on her own ever since, and she knew what it was to be in the care of someone who didn't truly want you. She knew how it ended.

So yes, all things considered, she would rather die than become Matteo's consolation wife. Because she would only end up dropped off in the middle of a carnival with cotton candy as a poor substitution for love.

But she wasn't a child with nothing. And she didn't need to wait for pity treats. She was a woman. With money. With a mind of her own.

"You cannot leave me," he said.

"I can," she said, feeling buoyant now. "I will. And I will not marry you, Matteo. Not for anything." She collected her coat, and her purse, and then she swept out of the office, a smile curving her lips.

And she had to wonder if Matteo had ever heard of the mouse that roared.

CHAPTER TWO

"WHAT DO YOU mean she's gone?"

All of her planners were still there. He had checked. And every single personal item in her room, except a shelf full of books, and a small jewelry box, was still there.

"She's gone," Javier responded.

His brother was lounging indolently on the chaise in his and his wife's rooms.

"How do you know this?"

"Violet told me. She saw Livia scampering about the place and asked her what was happening. According to Violet, she looked quite sad, but said she had to leave."

"She can't leave," Matteo said. "She's my assistant."

"Your mouse," Javier said, his tone mocking.

He knew Javier was disapproving of the nickname. Found it demeaning. Javier didn't understand. *No one could.* She was more than an assistant and had been from the start.

"That too," Matteo said. "I gave her everything she has."

"Clearly not *everything*, as she has backbone enough to stand up to you, so she seems to have had enough to recommend her all on her own."

"You know what I mean. She said she quit, but I didn't believe her. She left her planners."

Javier lifted a brow. "Well, she doesn't need them anymore."

"How am I supposed to know where I'm supposed to be, or what I'm supposed to do?" He waved his arm over the space. The space that was empty now. Void of schedule and direction.

Livia's organization was more than a convenience. It left him able to focus on what needed to be done in a world where his waking hours consisted of wall-to-wall work and his sleeping hours were not guaranteed because of the nightmares that often plagued him. Which meant half the time he didn't sleep.

Half the time he chose to spend the early morning hours in the gym, punishing himself. Because at least then the pain came from something real and not the deep dark of his psyche and memories of an old man long dead.

"She left her planners," Javier pointed out quite unhelpfully.

"I am aware. I'm the one that told you," he bit out. "I proposed marriage to her."

"You *what*?" That brought his brother up out of his lounge.

"I proposed marriage to her."

"I had no idea that you felt that way about her."

"*What* way?" There was no one way he felt about Livia.

"That you... You don't, do you?"

"I have said to you an abundance of times that a king has no room in his heart for love. As you well know. I do not have—I cannot have—softer feelings for anyone. Livia was a sensible choice. She already organizes everything in my life, she would be a fantastic asset to the country. Just imagine the sort of charity events she could pull off. She already does the essential function of a queen."

"Except warm your bed. And potentially provide you with heirs."

That stopped Matteo short. He had gone out of his way to deny any thoughts of his bespectacled mouse in his bed. And over the years...

He had little in the way of conscience, but he had a chosen code of honor. And being with Livia that way, given her position, would have violated it in every way.

But of course, if she were Queen, that would be part of the job description. Truly, it was the most important part of the job description. Because if he did not need to produce heirs, he would not need a wife. He would just as soon prefer to not have one, as a point of fact. His bloodline was tainted, and that he was Royal made it so he had to carry it on, and he found that... He did not care for it as a tradition.

His father had been an evil man. The things he had done to Javier, the things he had manipulated him to do... It was evil, pure and simple. That Matteo had not been able to protect his brother from his father's ill-treatment ailed him. But of course, he had endured his own trials.

Bedding Livia...

A kick hit him hard in the gut.

He had trained himself to find that response to her abhorrent. He had known her since she was a girl. He had rescued her.

He imagined her as she'd been earlier, those wide eyes looking up at him, her mouth pink and lovely and disapproving. And he gritted his teeth.

"It is practical."

"I cannot imagine why she turned you down."

"She was being unreasonable."

"Livia is *never* unreasonable. And you and I both know it. You, on the other hand, have cornered the market on unreasonable, at least, when it comes to this palace."

"Says the man tasked with fetching my fiancée, and then stole her."

"And you didn't care. Just like you don't really care that Livia won't marry you. You're inconvenienced and that's what you don't like."

But that wasn't it. It wasn't. He was not simply reacting as a man inconvenienced. He was not half so petty.

"Yes, you are," Javier said.

He met his brother's gaze, and did not ask him if he had said that last thought out loud.

"She asked if I was going to throw her in the dungeon for refusing. And as you know, generally when a king issues a commandment…"

"*Issues a commandment?* I thought you said you asked her to marry you."

"I did. By which I mean I issued an order that she would. Which when you are king is the same thing."

"It is not. And you, my dear brother, are out of touch with reality."

"Well, the next time I want the opinion of my younger brother, I will ask for it. But I do not believe I asked for your feelings."

"No. And indeed, only one person wants those. My lovely wife, who also didn't want to marry you."

"I cannot imagine why. I'm a nicer person than you."

"You lie better than I do. That's it."

Matteo let that settle in his chest for a moment.

"It is not a lie to behave in an appropriate manner in the appropriate venue. I am simply a man who knows when to put on the mantle of king."

"And I imagine Livia knows you a bit too well."

"Did Violet say where she had gone?"

"No. But I do not believe she said."

"Well, I will track her down, then. She cannot leave without it being on record. And I will find that information quickly enough."

"But she clearly does not wish you to know where she went," Javier said. "Perhaps you should respect that?"

"I have cared for her for nine years."

"She has cared for you. And anyone with eyes can see that."

"I will find her." He turned around to face his brother. "Where is your wife?"

"Do not bother her," Javier warned. "She's tired. Pregnancy is taking its toll on her."

"Congratulations. But I need to speak with her. And I am absolutely certain that she's hardy enough to handle it. Your great tragedy is that I have met her."

Javier rose from the chaise and went to the door that connected the antechamber and the bedroom.

"*Querida*, my brother wishes to have a word with you."

"Well, excellent."

Violet emerged from the bedroom, beautiful as always. She did not stir him, though. She never had. In fact, his interest had been…low. He did not worry over it, as he did not spend a large amount of time questioning his own motives, if any. He had no need of introspection.

"You saw my mouse earlier. Did she say where she was going?"

"I did see her. And Livia did not say where she was going. Only that she was."

"And you didn't stop her?"

"No. She seemed very upset and I can only assume that you were responsible."

"Yes, I was responsible. By proposing marriage to her."

"What he means is," Javier said, "he commanded that she marry him."

"Same thing."

"It's not," Violet said. "Having been on the receiving end of one of your proposals, I can tell you that it's not." She frowned. "It does surprise me that she would refuse you…"

"Thank you," Matteo said. "I find myself shocked."

"Please don't encourage him," Javier said. "His ego already needs its own wing."

"And we have the room for it," he said, his tone flat. "Especially now that Livia has vacated. Though I find it unacceptable, and I wish for her to return."

"Well, what were her objections to the marriage?"

"She made no specific objections. She only said no."

"It seems to me that she does not believe that marrying you has sufficient advantage. If I were you, I would focus on ensuring that she feels there is an advantage."

"And how will I do that?"

"Go and find her."

"Go and find her?"

He did not chase after people. Not anyone. Much less his assistant.

"If you really believe that she is the best choice for Queen, then I think you should."

Yes. That was actually not a bad idea. For she would marry him. She would see that he was correct. She was the best choice. And now that he had hit upon her as the ideal Queen, he could see it no other way. It would be Livia; it would have to be. He had given her a home, a position. Now he would give her a title, a family name. And she would give him heirs. Yes, he was determined in this and he would not allow her to defy him.

If his mouse thought she could escape him, she had better think again. For while she might have an extraordinary backbone, she was still prey.

And he was, as ever, a predator.

Livia had never had a place of her own before.

Once, she'd had a box. It was entirely hers. Centered in the middle of an alley. It had lasted two full days until moisture had encroached in the material and rendered it soft and useless. She supposed that didn't count, not as something of her own. Not really. But this apartment…

She stood in the empty space. The wood beneath her feet was scarred, the ceiling high, the windows tall and slim, facing out over the Seine River.

She'd been to Paris many times with Matteo. As

his assistant, his background accessory shrouded in black. But now she stood there in her Parisian apartment, quite her own person. It was a small place for she had money but didn't see the point in wasting it all on a massive dwelling that she had no use for. There was a living area, a kitchen, one bathroom and one bedroom. It was all she needed.

This felt very much like coming to the palace for the first time had. Oh, she could remember that well.

She had been so downtrodden. Angry, frightened.

For whatever Matteo had said, she deeply distrusted him. He was the new ruler of the country and he had done nothing to prove that he was anything unlike his father.

The former King of Monte Blanco had been a monster, and there was no other way to view that. He had made a game out of tormenting her people. A small cluster of indigents who lived in the old ways, who moved around, following the seasons. They had been poor. Hideously so. She wondered sometimes if her mother had spent the last of her coin on that cotton candy. A sugary sop for her guilt.

She also wondered if her mother had been able to return to their people. For abandoning a child in such a manner would be seen as beneath contempt. They had been a poor people, but proud and rooted firmly in family. That made it worse, really. She could remember trying to go back. She had walked for days.

But her people had moved on, and there was nothing but fire rings to denote that they'd ever been there.

And she just hadn't had the strength to walk on.

During the warmer parts of the year, they went higher into the mountains. Children rode ponies and in the backs of carts. She had gone to check one last time, the next winter, and they had not gone back to their usual haunts. She had known it was the fault of the King. There were talks of uprisings within the community. Men had disappeared. And her people had slipped away, not to be easily seen, and certainly beyond the reach of a ten-year-old girl.

In spite of herself, in spite of all that fear, she'd had no choice but to hope when Matteo had first brought her to the palace.

"This will be your room."

"*My* room?" She was filled with wonder in that moment. And for that moment she chose to feel nothing but awe.

"Different arrangements may be made in the future, depending."

Her awe immediately shifted to outrage. "I will not share a room with you."

He laughed. And it cut her somehow, even as she stood there wrapped in nothing but old clothes, pride and indignity. "I would not dream of asking. For I do not share my bed with girls. Particularly not girls that look like half-drowned mice who have not seen a morsel of cheese for weeks. But I will find you work here at the palace. There is always work to be done. You will have a position here for as long as you may need it."

"I will?"

"Yes."

"I…" She looked around at the glittering, gilded walls, the plush bedding. She had never in all her life seen anything like this. It was beyond her experience. Beyond her wildest dreams.

And this man, who had the face of an angel, all sharp cheekbones and dark eyes, black hair pushed back off his forehead and a smile that could not be described as kind, but not wicked either, looked as if he had been pulled from other dreams entirely.

"What is your name?" he asked, an intensity to the question that burned right through her. How long had it been since anyone had wanted to know? Whatever his reasons, he was asking after her and that felt something of a gift.

"Livia."

"And have you a family name?"

Bitterness clamped down in her chest and she lifted her chin high. "I have no family."

"Livia," he said. "A nice name."

She kept that compliment and turned it over in her heart. Livia. He liked her name. Bit by bit, she grew in strength. She found that she enjoyed work at the palace. There was cleaning involved, of course, but she found that she quite enjoyed making things shine. She found she had a talent for catching small details. She knew that she sometimes annoyed the more senior members of staff, but she was just so very…happy.

That was what had marked the first weeks there. *Happiness.*

She had spent years, the tenderest parts of her childhood, into burgeoning womanhood, existing in a space where she could barely make any progress. Where the best she could hope for was survival. And here she had found an existence that allowed her to embrace beauty. There was a simple sort of joy in polishing silver until it gleamed. In the excess that she found around her. The luxury of making things beautiful just for the sake of it.

And somewhere in the back of her mind she knew that her people would scoff. That all of this excess and indulgence was somehow contrary to the life that they had forged for themselves, but she didn't care. She had been betrayed by them.

She had been betrayed by her mother. She had lived a life of austerity, so why couldn't she enjoy the clean, fine clothes she was able to put on every day. Nothing fancy, a simple uniform of black pants and a white shirt, but the fabric was not scratchy, and everything fit perfectly. She was never too cold, she was never too hot. She was no longer at the mercy of the elements.

For weeks, she avoided going outside at all. For

why should she? She had lived outdoors for years. She was tired of it. She could stay inside where the man-made air could flow over her skin at whatever temperature she wished. Her room had its own controls.

Yes. She was bathing in luxury and loving it. The food that the staff at the palace ate was divine. It was the same thing that the King ate. She didn't mind that they were the leftovers off his table, not at all.

For the first time in her memory she went to bed, and her stomach was full. She was comfortable for the first time in years. She had forgotten what comfortable felt like. She was nearly oppressed by it. Because there wasn't a moment that went by that she didn't feel aware, that the fabric against her skin felt good; that she was not shivering; that she was not sweating.

And then there was the King. His presence. She felt it everywhere. Like a silken robe that she wore on top of everything else. She was simply aware of him, was in full wonder of him at all times. And she knew that the other maids—for they were maids, as easy as it was to try and think of her position as something a bit less servile—found her silly, that she was quite so in awe of the man.

But they didn't know what it was like to live as she had. And King Matteo was her savior.

"Are you finding everything here to your satisfaction?"

One day he stopped her in the ballroom, where she was shining the golden tiles of the floor on her knees, going over and over them until she could see her reflection in the brilliant surface.

"Yes," she said. "I find that I very much enjoy the work."

"My head of staff says that you always do more than is asked of you. But you spend a bit too much time on details for her liking. That you do not see the big picture."

Terror rang through Livia. "Oh. Well, I... The details make up the big picture, Your Majesty, with all due respect. You cannot have a glistening vista if the pieces that make it up do not sing."

"I agree with you, Livia," he said, the usage of her name sending a whisper of sensation over her body.

"But I can work differently if Mrs. Fernandez wishes."

"No. I wish for you to do whatever it is seems best. What sort of details interest you?"

"Oh. I don't know. I suppose it's just... The small ways the world is put together. I've always had an eye for detail. I've a very good memory. I'm quite fascinated by the way things come together, and I never forget. It has been useful to me in my life, living on the streets. I can remember faces, I can remember people, and avoid them if need be. I can picture an object in my mind, and try to figure out how I might re-create it with the things I have available to me. For I can simply see the way something comes together."

"Interesting. And when it comes to events? If you

were to fill this ballroom with people, can you see how they would fill the space?"

"Yes." She looked around the room, this room that she had learned from top to bottom in her time here. This room she had labored over. Every ornate piece of molding, every pane of crystal on the windows. Every tile. "Yes. I can see how you might furnish it for a function."

"Fascinating." He looked at her, with those too-keen eyes that made her feel seen. "What a strange little brain you have."

She looked away. "I've had nothing to do really but focus on the small moments for years. Thinking too far ahead when you live on the streets is only ever depressing. A long life of the same sort of thing looms ahead of you. So you must reduce it. You must take it down to small moments. If you don't, you'll go crazy. You have to find joy in small things because small things are all there is."

"Well," he said. "I can use someone to focus on such small things. For I must keep mine larger. I might find a *captain of small things* to be useful."

She brought herself forward to the present. It did no good to think about such things. Of those days, when she'd been his *Captain of Small Things*.

Her eyes filled with tears. It did no good to mourn Matteo. He had only ever found her useful. And that was it. He was scarred. Too scarred by his past to love. She knew that. And she was…

What was she?

She was a sad girl who had never truly grown out of her hero worship. Who had been given an extraordinary gift, and had focused on the wrong bit.

This was the takeaway. The ability to have this life. The ability to make something of herself. The ability to live in Paris if she chose. To be all that she could be. This was her life and all that she carried inside of her. Matteo should never have been her focus.

Matteo.

She didn't even think of him as King Matteo. Hadn't for years.

Well, now she wouldn't think of him at all. She was free of him. Finally.

She took a resolute breath and turned, and then her heart stopped.

She had heard nothing. Not a sound. But there he was, as if spirited there by magic. Standing in her doorway, broad, imposing and angry.

He was wearing a black suit, cut perfectly to outline the muscular lines of his physique. Expertly tailored, practically sewn on to ensure that it fell along the perfect lines. She knew, because she had been in the room when he'd been fitted. Had watched as he stood there, bare chested with measuring tape going over each part of his perfect form.

Oh, that had been a study in torture.

That was when she had learned about desire, and desiring a man. In Matteo's untouchable, awe-inspiring presence. He was across a room from her but may as well have been in another galaxy.

Men, in her experience, had been sources of fear. But there, with his stunning male beauty on display, she'd learned that there was more to men.

And as a result, her feelings on the matter had taken root deep inside of her and refused to let go. She did not have an attraction to men in general.

She had one *to him*.

But she was in Paris. She should be able to find a rakish, disheveled-looking man who was dangerously handsome and looking for nothing more than a good time. A man who could teach her that any man's body would do so long as it conformed roughly with her aesthetic preference.

Thinking about that seemed laughable with Matteo standing there.

She blinked once, very hard, just to make sure that he wasn't a hallucination of some kind.

He was still there.

"Paris?" His lip curled. "I did not take you for a romantic, Mouse."

She crossed her arms and fixed him with her most formidable glare, over the rims of her glasses. "I didn't take you for a stalker, Matteo."

"Are we on a first-name basis again? It was all very *Your Majesty* the day you left."

She lifted her chin. "I no longer work for you. Not only that, I'm no longer in your country."

"Your country as well."

"Not really." She thought again of her people, who she endeavored to not think of overly much. But she had been. Had she ever truly been part of the country?

"You have emigrated, then?"

"Clearly." She sniffed. "What are you doing here?"

"I've come to collect you." He looked around the space, disdain writ large in his expression. "Your tantrum is unwelcome."

"Oh, it's not a tantrum. It's called moving, I see it."

"That is not how I see it." He walked farther into the room. "In fact, I take a dim view."

"I hate to break it to you, but you do not make the rules of the universe. You do not get to decide what I feel."

He leveled his disdainful gaze onto her now. "You are acting like a child."

"*I'm* acting like a child? You've chased me down across country lines to bother me more about a question I gave you a definitive answer to. Not even a question," she said, laughing in spite of herself. "You truly are an arrogant bastard."

"Not a bastard. Legitimate. Arrogant, maybe, but not a bastard."

"I meant in the colloquial sense."

His eyes went sharp. "What will it take?"

"What?"

"What will it take to get you to agree to be my bride? There is a price for everything," he said, taking a step toward her. "If you don't, I'll believe you're holding out for a better bargain…"

"I am doing no such thing," she said, horror stealing through her. "I am not in the market to trade my body for anything."

"I'm not suggesting you become the palace whore, Mouse, I am suggesting you become my wife."

"Queen Mouse, ruler of your schedule." She waved her hand in a grand gesture. "Grand Duchess of your daily routine. Chancellor of your meetings. How could I resist?"

"Mother of my children."

She felt like he had shot her in the stomach with an arrow. So deep and hard was the pain that ran through her body. It resonated between her thighs, around her heart. Oh, she wanted to kill him.

There were no weapons handy in this empty apartment.

This was a farce.

She had not anticipated him playing quite so personal. For she had thought that if anything, he would go straight into his brand of logic, as he was a big fan of his own reasoning. But no. He had brought up children.

Oh, she wished that she could…

"The fact you consider that an enticement says a lot about you."

"What life do you think you'll have here? You could be like everyone else, I suppose. But you're *not* like everyone else, and we both know it. You are gritty and strong, it's true. You are resilient. Brilliant. Far too brilliant for most men, don't you think? I do. I think most of them wouldn't know the first thing about how to handle you."

"Your concern for me and my future is touching. And you obviously think…"

"It has nothing to do with me. And everything to do with you. Don't you think that after everything, you're worthy of a position as Queen? What are your concerns, Livia?"

Her name. When he used her name she…

"My concerns?" She cut her own thoughts off.

"Come now, surely you must have them? You come from a very particular position in life. You must see flaws in the system that I don't. You're correct, I'm arrogant. I'm a product of my environment. Resolutely and deeply, and I have never pretended to be anything else. I am suited to my position. I spent all of my life training for it. But my father was not concerned with the plight of his people. He made it worse. He plunged them into poverty. And you were swept up in that. You well know it. So tell me, what things am I overlooking? What causes could you spearhead in your position that you would otherwise be unable to do? How much more would you contribute than a woman of a different sort?"

"Yes, you're very concerned about this now, but you made a card table bargain with Violet King's father for her to be your wife. She's the daughter of a rich man who has made herself even richer. Where was your concern for the sensibilities of the impoverished at that time?"

"I wanted her American sensibility. For they are a country with flaws to be certain, but the perspective of someone from a family of those who have been self-made... I thought it would be useful. But you... You, Livia, are even more self-made."

"I was plucked off the street by your royal hand, Matteo. Surely you don't truly mean that I made myself."

"I think you have. Because it was you who caught my attention, you who moved through the ranks of staff at alarming speed. You and your brain that inspired me to promote you to assistant. Yes, Livia, I would say that you are self-made."

"Careful, if you keep referring to me by my name, I might start to think that you see me as a *woman* and not a *rodent*."

He frowned, staring at her for a long moment. "Is that what you think? That I see you as a rodent?"

"You call me *Mouse*." Such a love/hate relationship she had with that too. For he had nicknames for no one else. No one but her. He had casual endearments for his women. He called his brother by his name.

Only *she* had a nickname.

It was just an ignominious one.

"I'm the lion," he said, his voice soft but firm. "Didn't you know?"

Something hollowed out in the pit of her stomach, and this was where she despised herself. Because she was truly unable to resist that. Unable to stand firm in the face of such naked flattery.

His attempt to spin the interactions between them going back years. That somehow she meant something to him, mattered to him. Oh, she wanted to throttle him.

"Get out of my house, Matteo. For the first time in our interaction, I am not under your roof. And I do not need you."

"But Monte Blanco needs you."

"That's too bad. Because I need to become something else."

"Give me a chance." And for the first time in her memory…his arrogance broke and he had truly asked for something.

"Give you a chance to what?"

"Prove what manner of husband I will be to you."

And then, he closed the space between them, wrapped his hand around her neck and drew her forward. Then his lips came crashing down onto hers.

CHAPTER THREE

HER MOUTH WAS a revelation, and on some level, he must have always known that it would be. No matter how he denied it. Told himself it would be a base, treacherous act, he had known. For he had been fascinated by that mouth and the many moods that she could convey with a twitch of the corner of those lips. Amusement, disdain, irritation. He had learned to read that mouth, and now he was tasting it.

Feasting upon it.

Livia.

Livia, the one woman who had ever…

It brought his mind back. To that night.

Just before she had become his assistant. Still, then, she had been nothing more than a mere palace employee. And certainly he found excuses for their paths to cross, because he quite enjoyed speaking to the bright little creature, but they had not seen each other daily.

Until then.

* * *

He was in pain. Ferocious pain. He had never felt such pain. It was like knives being buried beneath his skin. And it didn't take long for him to realize that he was dreaming, to begin to try and push himself up into consciousness, from beneath the rolling waves of his subconscious.

Pain was all in his head. He knew that.

Unfortunately, the doctor that he had spoken to about the subject also made it very clear that pain—even when there was not a clear physical cause for it—was *real* because it always originated in the mind, and the body responded however it was instructed to.

And he felt it, keenly, when he had these episodes. A return to the torture that his father had subjected him to as a boy.

And when he awoke, he could feel a presence in the room. And he did not think. He did not bother to figure out the identity of the person in the room. No. He simply did what a warrior must do.

He attacked.

He launched himself from the bed, stark naked, as he always slept, and pushed forward to grab hold of the enemy. The enemy was soft and pale and small. The enemy did not break beneath his hands, but rather stood rigid, not running, not crying out, not begging for his life.

And then, it became clear that the enemy…was a woman.

"Your Majesty."

He knew that voice. He knew that voice well. Soft and measured, and no different than if he had asked her to report on the state of the palace.

"Livia."

"Your Majesty, I heard your distress. I was wandering the halls because I couldn't sleep and I…" Her breath pitched sharply. "If you wouldn't mind, could you remove your hand from my throat?"

He hadn't realized he'd been holding her thus. He released his hold on her and took a stumbling step backward, his chest heaving. "You do not have permission to enter my chamber."

"I know. And I apologize. It's only that I was cleaning. I know there's a big event tomorrow, and I didn't think that… There were things that I thought could be amended. And so I set out to do so. I was on my way to my room when I heard you. Are you all right?"

"Yes," he said, gritting his teeth. For the effects of the pain lingered. Psychosomatic though it might be, it burned.

"Can I get you anything?"

"Coffee," he said. He could send her away, but why? She had asked if he needed anything. And he would take her service. He was the King, after all, and he was in pain.

"Of course."

She scurried from the room, and he half expected her not to return. But she did. She was wearing her palace uniform, as if it was still the middle of the day, and not gone one thirty in the morning.

She turned the light on in the room. He was sitting with a sheet covering his lap, but he saw her eyes widen fractionally. She took two steps forward.

She was not trembling. Rather she met his gaze full on. But she did stop short of the bed.

"I will not harm you."

"Of course," she said, closing the distance and handing him his coffee.

"You did not make one for yourself?"

"I do not avail myself of the pantry outside of the hours the staff eat, sire."

"You should. You must. You're still far too thin."

Irritation twitched in her brows. "Forgive me, Your Majesty, but do you always pass judgment upon the physical form of those who work for you?"

"No," he said, "but I do find that I'm concerned for yours. You were quite poorly when I found you, I cannot forget it."

"No more poorly than I had been in any of the preceding years. I survived." She lifted a shoulder. "As one does."

"Unless one doesn't."

She frowned slightly as if considering this. "True. But I did. And continue to do so."

"Admirable."

"You have also survived," she said. And then she did something wholly unexpected. She sat down on the bed, not close enough to him that he would think she was making an attempt at seduction, but down at the end of it. A strange show of solidarity, he felt. Oddly unexpected and… He could not think of the last time a woman, a person, had sat with him in this way. Certainly not in a state of undress. Certainly not in the middle of the night.

When he was naked with women in his room, it was not to chat.

"I have nightmares," she said softly. "There were nights on the street when I did not think I would live to see morning. I slept with a knife in my hand, carefully concealed for I had to be ready. To wake up and stab an attacker if the moment presented itself."

His chest went tight. "And did it?"

"Oh, on several occasions. When the weather gets warm, things get difficult. When it is cold, people hunker down, go to their caves, certainly they avoid accosting women in alleyways. But summer… It was beautiful, and in many ways a more comfortable time to be homeless in Monte Blanco. For the weather here can be glorious. But… Yes, then you must worry about an increase of marauders in the street. And all that they might try and take from you."

"Did you ever consider living away from the city streets?"

She looked away from him, picking at thread on the blanket. "I did at times. But there you have the pressing concerns of wolves, bears. And my weapons, small as they are, are more effective against men. Men are much softer." She grinned, wide enough that he could see it through the darkness. "Though, I find wolves and bears to be less predatory, of a general rule."

"You do not have a high opinion of men."

"I didn't. But I had yet to see much of the good in them. You have given me something else to consider. I think you should be quite proud of that."

He didn't quite know how to react to that. It was a strange sort of compliment issued by such a low creature. He found that it warmed him. For it mattered, that he was not his father. For that man had been a monster; a man with no compassion in his soul.

And he had done his best to bleed Matteo of it as well.

Yet sitting across from Livia seemed to indicate that he perhaps had not succeeded. She was the first real indicator that perhaps his father had not had a complete victory in the war over Matteo's soul. Yes, he had purpose to be a fair leader, a good leader. One thing he had never understood about his father, though, was his comfort in being king of the trash heap. Would it not have been better to be king of a country with a thriving economy, with a reputation for caring for its citizens? Why hoard all the gold in your castle? Wasn't it better to behave as if the citizens of this nation mattered? He had never been convinced of his own goodness, he had merely determined, logically, to be different. Livia made him feel that perhaps there was more, and he wanted to hold to it.

"Tell me what you dream of."

"It is not a good bedtime story."

"Well, neither of us are sleeping. And neither of us are children. I wonder if I ever was one."

"I am the same," he said.

It was a strange thing, for he and his brother had both been raised by the same man, but they had been so very separate. Javier had endured his own form of pain brought about when he'd realized what a monster their father was. Matteo had always known. He had never been fighting the good fight of the king before him. It was the reason he had kept a wedge between himself and his brother, until Javier became suspicious of different war tactics he'd been asked to take, and his illusion of his father had been shattered.

Matteo never held such illusions. But Matteo had been the heir and his father had not been able to contain his cruelty in Matteo's presence. No. He had appealed to what he had seen as Javier's sense of honor, and had lied to him about the missions he led the military on. But with Matteo… He had sought to twist him in the same ways he was, and when Matteo did not comply, he was forced to endure physical torture.

His father had been so certain he could train into Matteo the kind of ruthlessness that he possessed. But Matteo simply did not yield. He *would* not.

In his dreams, though, sometimes he did.

"I dream of weakness," he said.

"Whose weakness?" she asked.

"My own. I have…withstood torture." He leaned backward, so that she could see the knife slashes that went across his chest. Then he turned his shoulder, so she could see where he had tasted the sting of the whip on his back. "I did not yield. I did not break. But in my dreams, sometimes I cry out. Sometimes, I am broken. And that is the final indignity."

"I'm sorry."

"There is no reason to be sorry for me." He inclined his head. "I am a king, after all."

She nodded. "But a man as well. I can see that in your scars."

"Reinforcing, perhaps, your theory that men are flawed."

"Oh, I know they are. But you've made me think, maybe they're good too."

"And what if I'm only good to further my own selfish ends?"

She was silent for a moment. "Do you intend to hurt people?"

"No."

"Then perhaps it doesn't matter why. I have lived

very selfishly for a great many years. Because I had to survive."

He nodded slowly. "I'm familiar with survival."

"Isn't it a wonderful thing, to live for more than that?"

He did not know how she remained so bright. How she had so much optimism.

"I never thought of it as such."

"I do. Every day. I think that's the real reason I get lost in the details of this place. It's wonderful to want something other than to not feel quite so cold. To not feel quite so hungry."

"Do you dream still?"

"Yes. That is something that's not quite fair, isn't it? The dreams are still there. But at least we both sleep in safety."

"Indeed we do."

And he thought of her then as a mouse, not because she was small, but because she was as the tiny creature who fearlessly approached the lion, and perhaps was the only one who could say what needed to be said or do what needed to be done. No one else had ever spoken to him quite like this. Perhaps because she was a street urchin who was so outside of everything that held the kingdom together, she was quite so effective. All he knew was that he had never quite felt as if another person had understood him so keenly. And there was something healing about sitting across from her, and seeing how she sat with strength. How she had not responded to him with fear. That this creature, so filled with an appreciation for life that he did not feel, so placid in the face of danger, but never truly placid. She made him feel like he could see the best outcome for a person who had been through such trauma. And he didn't think he would ever feel as she did. But he could see the merit of one such as her, a person who had endured all she had, and still had emotion. Still had hope...

He could see how it might be valuable to use her.

As the heart that beat outside of his body, for there was none to be found within.

Her lips brought him back to the moment, a shocked sound escaping her mouth. It was soft and sweet, and filled with desire.

Yes. He had known it then, and he knew it now. That she could be his heart. She could be the one who led with all that fierce conviction that she had.

She was the only one who could be his Queen, and if he had to seduce her to see it done, then he would.

Women enjoyed his body. He was not conceited about it, but neither was he falsely humble when it came to the assets that he possessed that women enjoyed. Why should he be? And so he kissed her. Kissed her until she cried out and stepped back. "What was that?"

"If you're going to be my Queen and produce my

heirs, we do need to know if we are compatible on that score."

He was honestly shocked as the desire that he felt for her poured through his veins.

He had not expected to feel this deep, low pull of attraction, not for his mouse. But then, she had always had a way to the core of him. She had always seemed to know him. And perhaps there was something in that. Perhaps in bed they would know each other in a way that proved pleasurable for them both.

"What makes you think you can manipulate me with sex?"

"Perhaps I'm not trying to manipulate you, Livia."

"No, I think you are. You're a man who does not like to be told no. And so, you chased me down, not because you want me half so badly, but because you cannot stand that I refused you."

"That isn't true."

"Don't argue with me. Do you know... I knew you were going to propose to me."

That stopped him. Cold.

"You... You knew?"

"Oh, yes. From the day that your engagement to Violet King was broken off I knew that you would be asking me next. Because I am practical, and I am sensible, and you want nothing less than what you want at all times, Matteo."

"I am a king, I'm not predictable."

"Maybe not to other people, but you are to me. This isn't about me. It's about having your way."

Anger burned through his veins. "Perhaps you have forgotten. Forgotten what I really come from. Forgotten who I really am. I am a man who has had no luxury of ruling with his heart, for I know how deceitfully wicked a person's heart can be. Perhaps you don't remember."

"Our late-night conversations about torture?" Her voice was quiet then. "Of course I do."

"Then before you write me off as an arrogant ass, perhaps you should recall that reality. I will not apologize. I will not apologize for seeking to do what is best for my country, and I will not apologize for limiting the danger that I posed to the world by cutting out my own heart."

"You have never been a danger to the world…"

"Of course I have been. You know nothing, Livia. Nothing of me. Not really."

"Arrogant even in your self-loathing. That you think so highly of yourself that you suppose you could mete destruction out upon the planet."

"You forget that I grew up with a monster. The only arrogance is believing that you are incapable of turning into such a thing yourself. That kind of arrogance is dangerous."

"All right. If that's what you need to believe."

"Let me take you to dinner."

The look she gave him was mean. "We go to dinner all the time."

"No. We don't." He looked around the space. "Where are you staying?"

"I'm currently in a hotel down the road, though I'm sure you know that."

He looked at her. "Of course I do."

"Then why did you bother asking?"

"I can't win. I'm either too arrogant or not arrogant enough."

"How tragic for you," she said, her tone arid.

"I will have clothes and instruction sent to the hotel."

"By whom?"

He smiled. "By me."

CHAPTER FOUR

LIVIA WAS STILL reeling over the kiss, and brooding over his actions, when there was a knock on the door to her suite. She had only had two hours' reprieve from him, and lying flat on her back in a dark room with a lavender sachet over her eyes hadn't been enough to quell her disquiet.

She had never been kissed before.

She hoped he didn't know that.

She would be *furious* if he did.

Absolutely *livid*.

Of course, she had no idea when he would think that she had had a sexual interaction of any kind. Her entire life had been devoted to him. And before that, her entire life had been devoted to her own survival.

She was in a foul disposition.

She stomped to the door and jerked it open. And there he was, looking downright disreputable. He was not dressed in a formal suit as he had been earlier. Rather, he was wearing a white shirt and no tie, the top button undone.

She had seen him nearly naked before.

And in fact, that night when she had gone into his room... He had been naked when he'd grabbed hold of her, but the room had been dark, so it had limited what she had been able to see. Still, over the years she had seen him in a bathing suit, in various states of half-dress as he wandered around, and she never got used to it.

His body was stunning.

A finely honed weapon that made a hard pulse go off between her thighs. And then there were his scars... She couldn't see them and not think of that night. The night when she had found out the two of them, however different they were, might have more in common than she had with anyone else she'd ever met. And it was an impossible sort of thing, to believe that someone like her could be so like a king. But she felt as if she was. She felt as if they recognized one another. Though she did not feel particularly like they recognized one another now. Mostly, she just felt like he was being an ass.

"I brought you a dress."

"I have plenty of dresses."

Of course, she had left all but two back at the palace, and they were all black.

"I do not wish for you to wear your typical garb.

You are not to blend into the background. You are going out with me as a date. Not as an assistant."

"I…" As she had quit as his assistant, she had very little to say on the subject. It was very hard to argue. "Why?"

"You know why."

"You're infuriating."

She took the bag from him and stalked into the bathroom. From there, she unzipped the bag, and frowned. The gown was red. Bright red. She never wore things that drew so much attention to her. When she pulled it out of the bag she saw that the fabric was slinky. Silky. It would spill over her curves like water and offer barely any coverage.

She slipped the dress over her slight curves and looked in the mirror. It was a simple dress. Barely more than a slip, with a V-neck and thin straps. The cut was basic, skimming close to her shape, and she had to ask herself why in the world she had put it on. Her own worried expression looked back at her. She reached into her makeup bag and pulled out a tube of red lipstick she had never used before. She didn't really wear makeup.

She swiped the crimson color over her mouth, and then dusted a bit of glowing sparkle over her cheeks. She looked… Well, as ever like Livia.

She would not wear her glasses out tonight, however. She took them off, and put them in their case, then put her contacts in. She didn't often do that; she found she liked her glasses, they provided a barrier between herself and the rest of the world, and sometimes that felt good. Sometimes it felt necessary.

Her stomach twisted as she put her hand on the doorknob. And she was reminded painfully of the day when he had asked her a different question altogether...

She'd been at the palace for two years. For the first time in her memory, she'd celebrated birthdays. She had done her best to forget when her birthday was, so when Mrs. Fernandez had asked, it had been nearly painful to come up with the answer. But she had cakes and gifts, and it was such a wonderful thing to be surrounded by friends.

It was her birthday, and King Matteo had asked to see her.

A shimmering sensation radiated in her stomach. She was certain she was in love with him. It was a foolish thing, and she did know it. He was far too high above her for it to become anything, but oh, he made her soul sing. He had asked her to meet him in the garden. She was already dressed up, because she had her birthday dinner. With her wages, she had bought herself a pretty red dress and she hoped that he would like it.

She was not a girl anymore, after all. She was a woman now.

She had filled out a bit, both due to age and easy

access to food, and she looked much nicer, much healthier.

She pinched her cheeks a little bit for good measure before stepping out of the palace, and into the gardens. It was a warm evening. Summer. She had hated summer once. But she loved it now. "There you are," he said. "Little Mouse."

He had taken to calling her that, and she didn't really know why. He didn't have nicknames for anyone else, so it felt... It felt almost special. He did pay special attention to her; it had been noticed by the other members of staff. She did not live with them in their quarters; rather, she kept her room in the palace. It caused tension between her and a couple of the girls, but everybody else seemed all right with it. Anyway, they were wrong about him. He wasn't keeping her to use her.

Would it be such a bad thing if he did?

Of course, she did not want to be any man's mistress. Nor did she want to be a whore.

But you could never be a king's wife...

"Yes."

She waited for him to say something about her dress. To wish her a happy birthday. He did neither.

"I have something to ask you," he said.

Her heart leapt up her throat, lodging itself there. He was a dark, imposing figure out there in the night, backed by a black sky shot through with stars. She used to sleep under a sky like that. The vastness of night had been frightening for her, never beautiful.

With Matteo in front of it, it felt…different.

He brought the vastness down to earth. Embodied it. She could no more tame or touch him than she could one of those stars but… But he made her feel safe, too.

He made her want.

"Yes?"

"Livia," he said, his tone going grave. "I would like for you to be my personal assistant."

Her heart stalled, then started again, slamming inelegantly against her breastbone. "Oh?"

"Yes. You see, I've been watching you, and I particularly appreciate your attention to detail. Plus… I don't know. You… You see things. It's not just details. You see things, and I need someone in my sphere who does. I need someone strong. Strong of opinion, strong in action. You will be my assistant, yes, but also my…advisor of sorts."

"Oh."

It was an incredibly flattering thing. But it was very far away from what she had hoped, for one brief moment, he might ask.

"I will of course pay you handsomely."

He named the salary that nearly made her double over.

"I don't understand what I've done to merit this kind of favor."

"Just being who you are."

And that was the shiniest, most glittering thing anyone had ever said to her and she took it and she held it close. And it wouldn't matter what else came after that.

"Now, I have sort of an unpleasant job for you, for your first task."

"Yes?" she asked tentatively.

She had no idea what he would classify as an unpleasant task, and frankly, it was a little bit disconcerting.

"I need you to select a farewell gift to my current mistress. Have it sent to her along with a note. Say something kind, but firm."

"I… You want me to…break up with a woman for you?"

"Don't be silly. It's a business arrangement, nothing half so feeling as 'breaking up' with. I never stay with a woman for longer than a few weeks. There's simply no way around it. If I stayed with someone for too long then I would have to start taking them to events, and I've yet to meet anyone who I would consider to be Queen. I have a prearranged marriage, you see."

And that was when all of her fantasies well and truly turned to dust. And that glittering thing she held close to her chest turned into nothing more than garden-variety craft glitter, which mattered not at all, and merely got all over everything and couldn't be gotten rid of, making a mockery of that feeling she had only a moment before.

"That makes sense. Of course, all of this has already been decided."

"By myself," he said. "An arrangement I made with an American businessman many years ago."

"I see. Well…" She knew she had a decision to make. She could feel sad that none of this was about her. That it wasn't about her birthday or her dress. That he was going to marry another woman. Or she could recognize the opportunity she'd been given for what it was, and grab hold of it.

"I'll take the job."

He smiled, and her heart leapt. She was a fool for him, and now she was about to be around him even more often than she already was.

"I didn't think you would ever refuse."

Oh, yes, she had been disappointed by Matteo while wearing a red dress before. And she could recall his confidence then, that she would simply go along with what he wanted. That she would comply with his commands.

She wanted to think she wasn't half so foolish now. Wanted to think that she had him completely and totally nailed down, and because of that, that there was no mystique left to him; and if there was no mystique left to him, he could no longer hurt her. But here she was, in a red dress, because he'd commanded it. With ferocity, she opened the door to the bathroom and walked out into the seating area of the hotel room, feeling defiant.

"Do I meet with your approval, Your Majesty?"

But there was something in his eyes then, entirely different than that night in the garden, that night when he'd asked her to become his assistant. There was heat there, and she felt an answering longing unfurl in her stomach. Of course, longing after Matteo was nothing new.

He kissed me.

Something shimmered low inside of her, that glitter that she would like to think had faded away years ago. But it hadn't. And this time it was different, because this time he'd kissed her. At least this time he was actually asking her to be his wife. It was just...

She wasn't that desperate street urchin anymore, and she didn't like to be made to feel like her. She didn't like remembering how weak he could make her. She wanted him; but he was a man who didn't love.

"Shall we go to dinner, *querida*?"

He had never called her *that* before.

"Don't call me that."

"It is, I think, an elevated term."

She shook her head. "Call me Mouse. That's what I am to you."

"Don't you think we should move on to something more intimate?"

"I don't. I don't, because at least Mouse is honest.

It's how you see me. It's what I am to you. A tiny creature you think you can put in your pocket and keep with you at all times. That's what you think I am. I'm not your *beloved*. All those blonde amazons you prance around with, *they're* beloved. For a night or two. I would have you be honest with me, at least. If you manipulate me, I'll know."

"And what?"

Ferocity boiled over inside of her. "I'll bite you. At the very least."

He took a step toward her, his dark eyes blazing with intent. "And what if I told you, Mouse, that I would not mind so terribly being bitten?"

"Don't tempt me, Matteo," she said, doing her best to raise her eyes and meet his.

Staring into those obsidian eyes now, she asked herself when that girlish love inside of her had heated to such an intensity, only to be cooled in such a way that it turned it into a hard obsidian.

Oh, it was still there. She couldn't deny her feelings for him. No matter that she knew better, it was just that she had learned to protect herself. It was the years as his personal assistant.

They had been instructive about the manner of man he was. He could put on a smile with the best of them—Livia had been the one to teach him to do so—but he was not truly a civilized man, and she knew it. She'd seen it. He smiled at all those women who passed through his life, passed through his bed, but it never reached his eyes. He was missing a heart, where other men had one. And she would do well to remember that.

"Come on, *Mouse*," he said, putting emphasis on the name. "Let us go to dinner."

CHAPTER FIVE

LIVIA WAS A VISION. On some level, he had always known she could be. Her hair was not demonstrably different than normal, tucked back in a low roll, with little wisps framing her face. But her glasses were gone, and he could see the stunning violet of her eyes with greater clarity. And that mouth…

Her mouth was a problem. Had been for years.

He had never seen it painted red.

It brought to mind a host of thoughts, none of which Livia would find appropriate. All the places on his body she might leave smudges of that lipstick behind. The way that her mouth might look if it was wrapped around his…

He shuttered those thoughts and put his hand low on her back. "Come," he said, "our car awaits."

Seduction was one thing, but he did not wish to overwhelm Livia with the depth of his depravity. He did not wish to overwhelm anyone with it. For he knew that a man such as himself had to remain in control at all times. A woman like Livia would demand it. She had lived through hell enough as it was.

One of the many reasons the attraction he felt for her was anathema to him for the last several years. She was vulnerable, and she was in his protection.

There had never been a moment where he might have found it fine to use her and discard her. Not after everything.

Proposing to make her his Queen was a different proposition.

She came with him willingly, but he could sense the reticence in every line of her frame. She was quite an elegant creature, really. He had appreciated a great many things about her, but he wasn't certain if he had ever appreciated that elegance. For she was small, and he tended to prefer tall women as he was quite a tall man himself. But every bit of delicacy that Livia possessed came together to create smooth, proud lines that shifted with grace as they made their way down to the lobby of the hotel.

The sports car he brought with him on his private jet from Monte Blanco was there, waiting in the front of the building for him. Livia looked at it, then looked at him. "Not our typical mode of transportation."

It was true. Typically, if he and Livia traveled together, he had a driver, and the two of them sat in the back of a limousine. This car was reserved for personal outings, and he and Livia were never on personal outings.

"No indeed. But I thought you might enjoy it."

"Some," she said, the sound an amusing one.

"What does that mean?"

"I only wonder why you think I would enjoy it."

"Why don't you get in." He led her to the passenger side, and opened the door for her. Then he got in on his own side and turned the engine over, the purring sound that filled the car one that never failed to send a thrill through his veins. He was a king, a ruler who had to keep his mind present at all times, and guard against the invading darkness left behind by his father. But when he drove, he was merely a man.

"I thought you might like it, Livia, because I believe that you secretly wish to go fast."

"Do you?"

"Have you ever ridden in a car such as this?"

She arched her brow. "I think you know I have not."

"Then trust me."

When he accelerated, he noticed her shift beside him, and he nearly smiled. The vibration of the car was sexual, it was undeniable. The way that the tires clung to the road as he maneuvered over the winding streets that led out of the city.

"And where are we going?"

"I see that you thought we might take advantage of one of the fine eateries in Paris, and while there are many to choose from, there is a private restaurant out here in the hills that I prefer. One that will allow us to indulge ourselves with a bit more privacy."

"Thus excluding you from the prying lenses of the paparazzi?"

"Not at all. They always know where to look for interesting photographs, don't you agree?"

"I suppose."

They continued the drive, the pastoral scenery blending into a green blur, and he focused on nothing more than the way Livia moved beside him, and the sound she made as he accelerated.

"You do like it," he said.

"That isn't fair," she said. "How could you possibly know I would like a sports car?"

"Because beneath all of your reserve, Livia, I do believe the heart of an adventuress exists."

"I've experienced a real fight for survival. I'm unmoved by these games played to feel like it."

"You are not, though. You are not unmoved by luxury, nor are you unmoved by a thrill, much as you would like to pretend you are."

"I don't see…"

"You are not the only one of us who knows the other. And I suspect you find that quite bothersome."

"Well."

"Well indeed."

Matteo felt thrilled that he had finally managed to silence the creature. Because of course he knew what Livia secretly wanted, down in her soul. She might pretend to be practical, but he knew otherwise.

He had seen her yearn for better things. For bigger things. He had watched her grow in confidence over the years. *He knew her.* Better than he knew anyone else. No point pretending otherwise.

Too soon they arrived at the château that would serve as a private dining area for them tonight. There were a limited amount of guests allowed in the château at any given time and, of course, heaven and earth had been moved to make way for him when he had indicated that he wanted to eat there. They served some of the finest food in France here, and given the culinary delights available in the country, that was saying quite a lot.

They pulled up to the front, and there was already a man waiting to handle the practicalities of parking the vehicle. Matteo himself went around to Livia's side of the car and opened the door for her, for he would not allow another man to attend to her in any way. Then he took her arm, and led her up the grand, cobbled walk into the ancient, stucco château. It was dimly lit inside, rustic wooden tables set about in the front of the building as they went through darkened halls, to a room that afforded maximum privacy. In there was an intimate wooden table, laid out for two. The chairs were clustered together, but there was ample space on the tabletop, for they would be served a grand feast, and he knew that the waiters made a habit of not interrupting, to the best of their ability.

"This is beautiful," she said softly.

She could not be cynical with him, which made him all the more pleased, because when Livia could not affect disinterest, he knew he had won. At least one small victory. She had liked the car, too, and she could not pretend with that either.

"Have a seat," he said, pulling the chair out for her. She complied, and he sat across from her.

There was something about the moment that brought him to another time, and as the food began to come out on ample trays—beautiful fruits and cheeses, homemade baguettes, local honeycomb and house-made pickled vegetables—it all faded away.

"The biggest issue that you have," Livia said, looking at him earnestly through her round, gold spectacles, "is that you come across as a bit of the beast. And if not a beast, then disinterested."

"That's because I find most people uninteresting," he said, leaning back in his chair at his desk.

Livia paced the length of the floor in front of him.

"But you want to begin to truly open up the country. To change things from the way that your father ran them, and that's going to require that you become a different sort of diplomat. And *that* is going to require that you become diplomatic."

"I suppose. But I am royal, is not my presence enough to sufficiently engage those around me?"

Livia rolled her eyes. She rolled her eyes at *him*. As if he was not her boss and her king.

"You will have to attempt to be a human being, Matteo."

"I must be human enough, for you have just called me by my first name."

Her cheeks colored. "Forgive me. I forgot myself."

"You forget yourself quite often, I find. Constant demands from someone in my employ, when it should work the other way around."

"Trust me on this, if you can trust nothing else. Trust that my perspective is from one who is not Royal. People need to see some humanity. When you go out and meet them, you need to be engaged. You need to… Smile. You need to at least pretend to listen to what they're saying."

"I'm sorry," he said. "I wasn't listening."

"You are maddening," she said. "Absolutely maddening."

"All right. I was teasing you. And I apologize. I will make an attempt at this civility that you speak of."

"If you really want to separate yourself from your father, it's not enough that you have a good heart."

He felt a strange, painful feeling squeezing around his chest. "I do not have a good heart. I don't have one at all. I find that is the best way to make sure you remain uncorrupted."

"You rescued me. You can't be all bad."

"I'm not," he said. "As I said. If you have no heart at all, then you cannot love power either. You cannot love yourself quite so much that you would put your needs above those of your own people. That is what my father did, Livia. As you know."

"Then what drives you? What makes you decide to do the right thing?"

"The knowledge that doing the wrong thing causes more damage than you could possibly imagine. The knowledge that the alternative is a wasteland of pain for all involved."

"Then get very used to figuring out a way to convey what I know about you. Which is that you have integrity. Will you agree with that?"

He inclined his head. "I will agree."

"It is not enough to simply act that way in private. You must actually show that you're a good leader."

"Are the people not fed? Are there not jobs? Have they not ceased disappearing from their beds for daring to disagree with me, or uttering a whisper of malcontentedness?"

"Of course they have. But people forget, their memories are short. The more comfortable you become, the smaller your complaints must be in order for you to feel badly. It does not take much to forget where you came from. To forget how truly bad things were. Take it from me. I used to sleep on the streets, and now sometimes I cannot sleep if I get tangled in the soft sheets on my bed."

The vision of Livia, tangled in her sheets, created a strange sensation low in his stomach. His assistant was growing more and more beautiful, it was difficult to deny. She was much different than the usual women he preferred, it was true, but there was a sort of delicate, bookish charm to her that he found fresh and appealing.

But he could also never forget where she had come from and the way they had come to know each other. He could not forget the position that put the two of them in.

He was engaged to be married. Or rather, an arrangement existed. Violet King would be his bride someday, and it had nothing to do with his feelings toward her at all, but simply what she might add to the kingdom. When he had made the arrangement with her father, it had only been out of consideration for what was best for the kingdom.

And one thing he could never do to Livia was...

He would never touch her. Beautiful or not.

He was pleased, though, to see how she had grown with health. To see her confidence. He found her a compelling, intriguing creature. This, he could not deny.

"Teach me, then."

"All right. Pick a topic that you're not interested in at all."

"There are so many," he said.

"All right," she said. "I will pick one for you. I have found that collecting hobbies is a wonderful side effect of having both free time, money and a lack of fear over your surroundings. I have begun doing needlepoint. I find something very soothing about it."

He could feel his eyes beginning to glaze over. He could think of nothing that he cared less about. Though there was something striking about the way her eyes lit up when she talked about it. Something about her joy that made him *feel*… Well, he did feel.

"Don't you think?"

That was when he realized he had not been listening.

"Of course," he said.

"You think there is nothing quite so diverting as watching golden thread slide through the muslin on a sampler?"

"Well, I imagine for you," he said.

"You weren't listening."

"No. But it's very boring."

She sighed. "And that is what you must not do."

"Livia," he said. "I appreciate that it means something to you."

"Okay," she said. "That's very good. So when you find yourself drifting off, perhaps you can find it in you to appreciate that."

And for the next hour, he did endeavor to listen.

And when he found it difficult, he focused on what it meant to her.

"So much better," she said. "Now tell me about something you like."

"Archery?"

She laughed. "Archery. All right. Why do you like it?"

"I like the thrill of the sound of the arrow flying through the air, knowing it will land at the center of its target. Knowing that I never fail. There is something intoxicating about seeing that. Seeing it and knowing it is so."

"Arrogant, but human."

"I am not a human, though, I am a king."

"It isn't about what you think. It's about what people will think."

"Why do you feel this so strongly?"

"Because I know what it's like, to be vulnerable. To be on the street. The idea that somebody strong is in charge, someone who might actually care for you, who has the heart of someone who would pull a girl from the street, and give her a new life... Oh, knowing that would have given me something to hope for. You don't think it matters—emotion, connection—but it does. Even if you cannot feel it, if you could show it, that would make all the difference in the world to the people who struggle."

"You are not wrong."

"Is that your way of saying I'm right?"

"I wouldn't go that far."

"Well, however far you would go… I'm glad that we could come to an agreement."

"I'm going to need you to come with me to this event. In fact, I believe you should come to all of them. Monitor my performance. Tell me how I'm doing."

"You want me to give you notes?"

"Yes," he said, "I believe I do. I think I would find it beneficial."

"Well…if you would find it beneficial…then… all right."

"Make sure you wear black, you will match the rest of the staff."

Those parting words echoed in Matteo's mind. He had truly said that to her. That she made sure she blended in. The problem with Livia was that, in his opinion, she didn't blend in easily. She was a distinct-looking woman, and she had been staff. So, it had been fair enough. Right now, she was not blending at all. She was eating bread and butter and the absolute joy in her expression was impossible to downplay.

"You are not so unhappy with me now," he said.

"Well, it's impossible to be unhappy when you're eating bread and butter."

"Is it?"

"Remember when you told me that I could make use of the pantry whenever I wanted?"

"Yes," he said. For he remembered every detail about that night. About their first real conversation. When he had been naked and drinking coffee, and she had perched herself on the end of the bed.

"It was a revelation. To be able to have food whenever I wanted. My life was never like that. Growing up, I..." She hesitated.

"Tell me," he said. For he didn't know anything about how she had grown up. He knew about her time on the streets, but not how she came to be there. Not even really how long she had been there. They had spoken of that part of her life, but not the time before it, and he'd always had the sense that it was the before that was all too painful for her to cope with.

"My family were..."

"I thought you said you had no family. No family name."

She shook her head. "Well, I didn't. After I was left on the street, I had no family. And anyway, my people do not have family names."

"You are one of the people who live in the old ways," he said.

"Yes."

There were those who had resisted the move to modern technology in Monte Blanco. Those who had resisted the monarchy. Who had preferred to live as they always had, in large extended family groups governed by themselves. His father had done everything he could to stamp them out. For in these groups there were often whispers of revolution. And anything his father could not control, he hated. These people were beholden only to each other. They cultivated their own ground, they made their own economy. It left them difficult to govern.

A fact that did not bother Matteo, but they had been heavily persecuted under the rule of his father.

"You never said."

"I do not like to think of it, for what is more important to those of the old ways than family? It is who we are supposed to be governed by, in allegiance to. Above the King. But I was left. So…"

"Yes," he said.

"Anyway. There was not ample food. Not always. It was finite, and there was not really currency exchange. We bartered and traded with others like us, and we grew our own food, farmed our own animals and hunted the woods. Feast or famine, that's how it was. But there was no refrigerator to simply open and find within it food of infinite varieties. Still, it was luxurious compared to the time I spent on the streets. I have never forgotten that. That moment when… Food, whenever I wanted it, whatever I wanted, simply became available to me. I love food." She laughed, the sound expanding something in his chest. "I really do. I love bread."

"I am pleased to give it to you." And he found it was true.

He had given women diamonds and been on the

receiving end of less gratitude. She still thanked him for bread.

It made him want to give her more. To shower her with things that he never had. Their relationship had always been…different. She had never been strictly his employee. But of course not, for she had been his advisor in many ways. He felt that all kings needed one, someone that they had some sort of accountability to. And while his brother served, in part, that position, what he had always liked about Livia was that she was not part of their toxic upbringing. She came at things from an entirely different perspective than they did, and he found that to be beneficial. But the fact remained that theirs had been a professional relationship. Sort of. They had not sat like this, and he had not personally given her things. Not personally chosen a dress for her or sat in an intimate dining situation. They talked always in his office, with the exception of that night. And with the exception of their trip only a month ago…

"Think of all the other things I could give you access to," he said. "Think of that change. Being able to open the fridge and have food whenever. Being Queen would give you doors you could open that you cannot possibly imagine just sitting here now."

"You act as if I might be swayed by the offer of power."

"Not power. Opportunity. I know you well enough to know power does not appeal." The rest of the meal came, and it was as divine as what had preceded it, and they quit talking, just sitting together in a companionable silence while they ate.

When they were through, knowing that there would be coffee and dessert coming soon, he looked at her, and he made the determination that he would continue this, as he would with any woman he had taken for a date. "Shall we dance?"

CHAPTER SIX

LIVIA DIDN'T PARTICULARLY want to dance. Because she didn't want to be quite so under his spell. From the moment he had put her in the sports car, and they'd gone whizzing out of the city, whipping around the tight turns on the road that led up to the château, she had been… She was feeling weak.

That was the problem. Because he was right; she did love the speed, and it was something she had never experienced. Because he did show her things that she had never even thought she would like, and he made them into something that felt essential. The problem was, Matteo had been engaged in a slow seduction of her senses for the past nine years, whether he knew it or not.

She had practice shielding her feelings, but it became complicated when all these other things were woven in. The food had been beyond anything, and she ate well. The food at the palace in Monte Blanco was fantastic, as was the food served at all the events that they frequented. But she had never sat down at a gorgeous restaurant and been served in this way. There had always been a division, and here she was being treated as an equal. Being treated as if she was one of those fancy, beautiful women that had always been in his sphere.

Not with that slight difference in their station that had always been there. More than slight. The fact that she had been given weight to her opinions was a testament to her job, not to anything else.

She was a girl from the streets, and before that from the woods. And she had finally told him.

And now he was asking her to dance.

She should say no. She should. But she had not danced with Matteo since...

"It is likely that you will need to learn to dance."

"Why?"

"Because we are beginning to do more and more events. Because the nation is beginning to blossom. And as you do attend all these events with me..."

"As staff," she said.

"Yes, but I think it would be beneficial for you to have the skill. Part of being cultured, and all that."

Livia cocked her head. "Your father prioritized you knowing how to dance?"

"It was considered a skill of enrichment that all royals should have. Part of what our au pair instilled in us. Things my father issued edicts about." He let out a bitter laugh, and it made Livia shiver. "You know, between bouts of torture."

"I wish he were not dead," she said. "For I would dearly like to kill him."

He laughed again, this time with a bit more mirth. "I do not doubt you would, Mouse. For you are ferocious if nothing else."

"I do not like injustice. I've experienced too much of it in my life."

"Sadly, injustice is all too common in the world, is it not?"

"Yes. Very sadly."

"Come," he said.

He extended his hand, and she looked around the office. "What?"

"Dance."

"There is no music."

"You do not need music. For it is all run on a very specific rhythm, these traditional dances. You can feel it. You can count it by your feet."

"That is not very… I mean, that's definitely not how I think of dancing."

"Because you don't do it. You do not know of which you speak."

His hand was still extended, and she looked at it quite like it was a snake that might attack her at any moment. But she was skeptical and suspicious of all of this. And mostly afraid of what might happen to her if he actually touched her.

"Livia," he said, and it was her name that enticed her to move.

Damn the man.

She took his hand then and electricity zipped through her body, and she was grateful that he quickly pulled her up against the hardness of his chest, for it hid the flaming heat that flooded her face, that she knew would be visible if he were to look. "Like this," he said, beginning to move. "One two three four. One, two, three, four." And with each count, a step, and a sweep of movement. He established a steady rhythm that carried her over the floor as if she was flying through the air, and all the music that she would ever need was inside of her. Flooding her, filling her, and then, she could no longer hide her face, because she needed to see his. She looked up, meeting his gaze. "Just like that," he said, his voice soft. "One, two, three, four. One, two, three, four. Perfect."

"This isn't so hard," she said, her voice trembling. Betraying her.

"It will depend on your partner, of course. For not all men have quite the skill I do in leading."

"So arrogant."

"One, two, three, four. Good girl."

Pleasure poured over her. Oh, she badly wanted to be a good girl for him. To be what he needed her to be. The things she felt for this man were... Well, they were beyond anything she had ever experienced before. And really, she hoped to never experience them again. She could scarcely stand it with a man who didn't much acknowledge her as a human being.

Sometimes, she felt she did not want it to be more. Did not want to take it deeper, and sometimes she badly did. But it didn't matter. Because it would never be anything. It never could. He was not teaching her to dance so that she could dance with him, but so she could blend and not embarrass him at an event if the opportunity arose.

That was all.

"One, two, three, four."

It got lost, though, in that steady rhythm of his beautiful voice. Oh, she truly was a lost cause, finding everything about him so enticing. She suddenly became aware that she could feel his heartbeat. Steady, like the rhythm he counted. Her own was not so steady. It was bouncing around erratically in her chest.

"Very good," he said, and it took her a moment to realize they had stopped moving, because everything inside of her was still spinning.

And then suddenly, as she looked up at his face, she felt something crackle in the air. Felt the thickness there, like a tension band being slowly stretched. And her heart jittered, slamming against her breastbone.

She could barely breathe. She could…

"I think that is enough for today," he said, turning away from her.

"Yes," she said, feeling dizzy and breathless and entirely out of sorts. "Quite enough."

"Shall we?"

"Yes," she said.

He took her hand, and led her away from the table, down the hall into a small, intimate room, where there were other couples. There was music playing and people were swaying together slowly.

He took her into his arms, and she felt that same thrill she had years ago, being held up against that big, solid chest. He had only grown broader and more solid with the passing years. A man who had grown exponentially in strength and character.

Of course, she would keep all that to herself, for it was a bit fanciful. But she never felt fanciful. Not really. But now, in his arms…

She just wanted to forget everything else for a moment. To forget the proposal, and why she had run. To forget that he didn't feel the things that she did.

To forget how much she feared being in a relationship where she was the one who loved, and the other one did not. Oh, why couldn't she just accept what he was offering? Accept the commitment, even without the feeling.

That made her feel strange and hollowed out and she decided she didn't want to think of it at all.

Not in the least.

So she pushed it aside and focused on nothing more than the precise feeling of where she was at the moment; the warmth of his body, the strength of his arms, the feeling of his suit jacket beneath her hands, and the heat and strength of the muscle beneath.

This wasn't a memory. It was now, and it was happening. He was dancing with her as he had done with any number of women over the years. With her dressed up, and with music. Not just counting off the rhythm in the privacy of his office while she was wearing her sensible uniform. Now, so much of her skin was exposed, and she felt every inch of it.

She didn't know how to feel about the fact that his touch didn't affect her any less now than it had when she was nineteen. That she could know all the many things she did about him, have years' worth of experience knowing him, living with him, caring for him, being hurt by him… How could she still be so enamored? She wanted to know better. Fleeing to Paris was her trying to know better. It really was. She had no desire to be a fool where Matteo was concerned, but there were times when she worried that there was simply no other way for her to be with the man, so it had seemed like the better part of virtue to leave. Completely.

But he had come after her.

And if she'd been thinking, really thinking, about the man that he was she would have realized that.

Did you not?

She ground her teeth together.

Really, Livia. You anticipated his proposal, but did not consider that he would chase you down?

Well, when she looked at it from the point of view of his arrogance, then perhaps she could see it. But truthfully, deep in her soul she had thought that his proposal would be born out of a sense of convenience, and chasing her down to Paris was not convenient. Not in the least.

Yet here he was, and here they were. And they were dancing. And his hands were warm and large, his arms were strong, and she wanted nothing more than to melt into him. Wouldn't it be wonderful to just lose herself completely this way?

Why did she have to think so much? Couldn't she just not think for a moment?

She thought all the time.

Remembered what she knew of Matteo's life, reminded herself not to fall too deeply under his spell, considered the optics of every interaction she had with members of state, and of the palace, and then Matteo's *optics* as well. Thinking had been what brought her here. Thinking had been the thing that had saved her.

And she had to credit it was quite a lot, all things considered.

But for a moment couldn't she just feel? Couldn't she just… Couldn't she simply be a woman in the arms of a man that she desired? Why shouldn't she have that? And really, when all was said and done, why shouldn't she have a little bit of...

Couldn't she have a little something for herself? Maybe she needed to leave him. She knew that she did. She knew that she needed to make a new life for herself. Maybe it would be at this apartment in Paris, or maybe she would move on.

Maybe she would go to Spain, or Italy.

Maybe she would go to the United States.

She loved America.

She loved California, and the endless coastline there. She loved New York, and the skyscrapers that seemed to build a glass-and-steel box all around you with just the barest window into the sky when you stood in the midst of Manhattan.

He had taken her to Wyoming once, to a ranch, to discuss some business deal or another, and she had been absolutely enraptured by the endless sky.

The world was opened to her.

She could not forget that to an extent it was open to her because of Matteo.

But it was also limited because of it. Because her feelings for him kept her in thrall.

You just thought it yourself. Your mind got you to all these places. All the things you did.

It was true. She had done a great deal of her own rescuing. She had needed to take his hand, and she had, but everything else she had fought for all on her own.

From the moment her mother had left her at that carnival she had been fighting for herself.

So why shouldn't she take the reward that she wanted?

Not his crown.

His body.

And so she let all of her thoughts fall away. Like the petals on a rose, wilting as time passed, inevitable, sad, but the way it must be. Shift, fall, as time marched on. The shape of all that beauty changing, passing away.

And yet at the center of it there was the truth: her feelings, her desire.

She wasn't a girl anymore, that much was true. Wasn't a starry-eyed girl who would believe that the King might find it in himself to love, just for her.

A woman who wasn't even suitable to be his Queen.

And this was not about suitability, but about Matteo's own need for convenience. She knew that. Violet King had been about suitability.

Neither one was particularly romantic, but at least Violet wouldn't have cared.

For Violet did not love him.

Of course, she had fallen in love with Javier, who Livia had always known had a heart beating beneath that iron exterior.

Matteo's brother was a warrior, openly. He had been a part of the battalion that had led devastation against her people. But she did not hate him for it. For he was a man driven by the burning belief in what he thought was truth. And once he had recognized the lies, he had gone in search of the truth, because he cared more about integrity than about any ideology.

There was a passion to that.

Whereas Matteo… He had always seemed so much colder. Cut off. Matteo was a different sort of thing altogether.

But he felt warm beneath her hands. There she could sense passion. There she could sense a man.

She moved her hand from his shoulders, down to the center of his chest, and beneath her palm she felt the beating of his heart. She closed her eyes for a moment and simply felt it.

For whatever he said about the presence of his heart, it was very clearly there. And she knew that he had meant it in a metaphorical sense, when he said he didn't have one, but the incontrovertible evidence that it beat just like it would in the chest of any other…

It made her feel resolute in this.

"You have grown into quite a good dancer," he said, his voice rough.

"You have never had occasion to know."

"Other than our lesson, no. But you did always move with grace, even then."

"Years of running and dodging foes in the streets, I would imagine."

"Ah, perhaps that explains my skill at it. Years of dodging my father's wrath."

It was so rare he would ever speak of this pain in such a casual tone. She knew about his past. She'd seen him in the throes of his nightmares. But it wasn't just…something to be spoken of plainly. Out in the middle of a dance floor.

She stared at the pulse pounding in his throat. "Probably," she said.

"We are not so different." His words were soft, and they wrapped themselves around her like a blanket.

She and a king, not so different?

Except she felt that sometimes. Like he might be the only person who matched the innermost part of her.

And it was foolish.

"No. Not so different. Only from different worlds. Might as well be different planets, honestly."

"You know we are not."

"Does it matter?"

He shook his head. "No. It is not about whether or not we are alike or different. But I believe you would be a good queen."

"Well, I thank you for your confidence in me. It is truly flattering."

"Am I not always?"

"Rarely. Never."

"Such flattery coming from you, Mouse."

She sniffed. "You know I never flatter."

"No," he said. "It's true. At the same time, you're the one who taught me to do it. Remember how you told me I needed to be human?"

"Yes. I do."

"Is that something you had to learn?"

She shook her head. "No. I had to learn to pretend not to be. To put away concerns about whether or not I had truly hurt someone with my knife when I was defending myself. To eliminate any guilt that I felt over taking a loaf of bread from a bakery. For they had many and I had none. I had to unlearn humanity, and coming back to the palace allowed me to find it again."

"A difference," he said. "I think."

"Yes. I believe so."

"You left your family when?"

Matteo was treading on new ground somehow, with each spoken word. They knew these things about each other. Information dripped into conversations over years. But they didn't *speak* of them. Not like this. Not with intention.

"My family left me," she said firmly. "When I was ten. But you make a good point. For ten years, I was happy. For ten years, I felt a sense of security, a sense of love. The fact that it turned out to be a lie doesn't erase it. And whatever my mother felt or didn't feel, there was a time when I was surrounded by the warmth of that family group. There was a time when I felt…cared for. You never felt that, did you?"

It was her turn to push. Her turn to make him share.

He shifted his hold on her.

"Not until my father was dead. And even then, it's not a sense of being cared for, it's just being able to control the environment that I am in. And the environment all of my people are in."

Her heart squeezed. She didn't want to feel so much for him, but she did. This man who'd had to learn how to show an interest in others because he didn't know *how* to show, not because he didn't know how to feel.

Whatever he thought.

"You had to show a level of care that was never extended to you, to others," she said, wanting to lean closer to him as she spoke, "and it is to be commended."

He made a scoffing sound. "None of it is to be commended," he said. "It's basic human decency, and even without the ability to feel much of anything, I can show it."

"Many people would choose not to. Has anyone ever taken care of you?" she asked, meeting his gaze.

His answer came quickly, firmly. "You."

"Oh."

They continued to dance without speaking and she let her focus go entirely to the way his arms felt around her, the way his body felt. He felt that she had cared for him. And she hated the way that it made her chest feel like it was broken open. Hated how much it made her feel. How she would like to be free of this. This desperate yearning inside of her. Hadn't she just purposed to try and embrace her attraction to him only to fulfill a fantasy? Well, perhaps it would work if *he* were simply a fantasy.

But the knowledge that she, and she alone, was where he had experienced care...

Little moments of their life shared passed through her mind, from that night they had sat together on his bed drinking coffee, to the times that she had left him notes on his birthday, quite apart from the vast gifts that he received from heads of state, just personal things. The way that he had done the same for her, at least after that first, disastrous birthday, where she had dressed in red and he hadn't known. He had found out later. And why? He claimed he didn't feel, but that was... It was feeling. It was caring.

He was a man with shields erected all around his heart. And she understood that. But she could also feel that same heart beating.

So she knew it was there.

Don't do this to yourself.

You came to Paris for a reason. You came to get away from him.

But she found herself leaning into him. Found herself stretching up on her toes and kissing his mouth. All that mouth. It held so many of her most dearly cherished fantasies. He tightened his hold on her, angled his head, his tongue sweeping between her lips, sliding against hers.

Her heart was threatening to beat right out of her body. Her pulse thrumming at the base of her throat.

Matteo.

Oh, Matteo.

She didn't say it out loud but his name filled her like a prayer, like a promise, echoing in the chambers of her heart, making it feel too large for her body.

Matteo.

They stopped moving then, and he gripped her chin, holding her face steady as he kissed her harder, deeper.

It was as if the room around them had faded into nothing, the people around them dissolving along with it. Because nothing mattered but this. This moment.

Don't get caught up in it. You have to remember. You have to remember.

"My brother tells me that he has made contact with Violet King."

"Oh?" Livia knew exactly who Violet King was. A makeup mogul, famous in the United States, and indeed the world over.

"Yes. She's my fiancée."

"What?" Her heart slammed against her breastbone.

"The woman that I have been promised to marry all this time, Violet King."

Livia felt her mouth drop open and close, and realized that she must resemble an indignant guppy and the last thing she needed was that kind of comparison floating around. She was already called a rodent half of her days. She didn't need to be a flopping fish. But she felt like one. Gasping and dry drowning in the air.

"Violet King is your fiancée?" The woman was younger than Livia. It was… Insulting.

Right. Because Violet King is a self-made billionaire and you are…?

A street urchin.

A street mouse.

Never, ever to be deemed appropriate to touch the sainted hem of Matteo's robe, let alone his body. Let alone… What did she even think? These fantasies that she had been so unsuccessful in staving off over the years.

But the problem was sometimes it was so easy to believe that they almost were an old married couple. One that didn't exchange endearments or physical contact, but they were downright domestic at times. Except that he was filled with arrogance and she with acerbic comebacks for his nonsense. So yes. That was a type of domestic, or at least, she assumed so.

But sometimes it felt like…like their lives were theirs. Like nobody else truly shared time with Matteo the way that she did. She saw him in the morning, she saw him before he went to bed. Sometimes she saw him after. She saw him barefoot, which was a decidedly intimate thing, she had determined. For he was a king, and she saw him without his formality draped around him. Saw him wandering his bedroom shirtless, wearing nothing but a pair of black trousers, his beautiful, muscled body shifting and rippling each time he moved.

She had seen him *brush his teeth*.

This man, who was nearly immortal. She had literally stood in his hotel suite while he stood at the bathroom sink and brushed his teeth.

Violet King had never seen him brush his teeth.

And Livia may not have so much as kissed him, touched him, but surely she was the only one who truly knew the man.

And what kind of unfairness was this?

A twenty-one-year-old socialite? Who did… *Internet posts for her job.*

And yes, made makeup. So, it was a real thing. And Livia was just being bitter. But she felt entitled to her bitterness. To her disappointment.

You knew it was coming. You always did. He made no secret of the fact that he was promised to another woman.

Why it should gall so much that it was an American, a young one, she didn't know.

You don't know? Of course you do. Because he is yours, and this is your country. Because it isn't even

Violet's country. She has no loyalty or allegiance to the throne, to the crown, not in the way that you do.

Even all that didn't really matter, because the real issue was Violet didn't love him. Not like Livia did. She couldn't.

But you're a fool, because he doesn't love you, and he has never pretended to. He has never loved you. He has never acted like he did. He has never so much as put a hand on you other than to teach you to dance.

To lift you from the gutter.

Her chest heaved with building disappointment, and she turned away from him to try and keep him from noticing. To try and disguise what was undeniably a sob.

"When will she be here?" she asked, pretending to be busy with papers on his desk. But her eyes were blurry and she couldn't see anything.

"Soon, I imagine. Javier said that she was not… amenable to the situation."

"What?"

"Oh, she didn't know, apparently. Which is the fault of her father…"

"So then… What?"

"Javier is bringing her here."

"Against her will?"

"Well, I don't know about all that."

"I think you do."

"Her will is not my concern."

"You…" She rarely fought with Matteo. She challenged him, but she did not yell at him, for he was the King, after all, and engaging in something like that was not proper. But, here she was. About to completely and utterly lose it. No, not about to. She *had* lost it.

"You arrogant bastard. You uprooted this woman from her home, from her country and dragged her here?"

"Is it really any different than what I did for you?"

That was like a knife straight through her heart.

"Yes. You brought me here and hired me as a maid. I had nothing, and you remind me of it constantly. You act like you saved me. But you know, the virtue of your presence doesn't save anyone, Matteo. The people in this country were saved, not simply by your hand, but the fact that you declined to bring it down upon them the way that your father did. And what they have chosen to do with their lives is what will save them. They have lifted themselves up with their own hands. Your father prevented it, more than you have ever aided it. Violet is a billionaire, of her own authority and her own hand. Not yours. And you are uprooting her out of a life that she built for what?"

"Her father promised her to me."

"This is not the twelfth century. What about her choice? What about what she wants?" And suddenly, she did not feel that she was talking about Violet. "You don't care about any of that, do you? You just want to assign roles to the people in your life. And all the better that your Queen be a woman who didn't even know that she was engaged to you. Who has no choice. You don't know her, you can't simply slot her into the position that you see her filling. It doesn't matter who she is…"

"She is well-liked throughout the world. I have seen her photographs. She is very modern. She is the kind of person who will bring the image of rehabilitation to the country that—"

"Kidnapping an American girl is hardly going to rehabilitate the image of Monte Blanco. Or your image. I thought… All these years I thought maybe I had done something in… Not just teaching you to smile, but teaching you to feel it. Not just teaching you how to pretend to connect with people, but to actually… But I didn't, did I? I taught you nothing. You… You don't feel anything, do you? You're a monster."

"I never claimed to be anything but a monster," he said, reaching out and gripping her arm, turning her to face him. "Did I? I just claimed that I was going to do my best not to continue the harm that my father caused. But I told you, all those years ago, you know."

"About your scars? Yes. I know. I know all about your scars, Matteo. You've shown them to me. But what does it matter if you've done nothing to try to heal from them?"

"They do not heal. It has been years, and there they remain." He tapped his forefinger against his temple. "And the pain stays there. And I feel it here." He touched his chest. And she knew that he was indicating the knife wounds there, but she wondered if he actually meant somewhere deeper. Though he would never admit it. "I am what he made me. Do you think I would not like to be? Why do you think that I debased myself to go and see a psychologist about the pain?"

His pain echoed inside her. Along with the gutting realization that perhaps she had not done a thing to make him...better.

She'd hoped.

She really had.

But it was possible he wanted too much. Demanded too much.

"It pains you that you're just a man, doesn't it?" she asked. "You wish to be immortal, but you aren't. You are just a man. And you have to contend with the failings, the limits of your body the same as the rest of us do."

"It should not be."

He was impossible. He really was. He wanted perfection and without it he would see himself as broken and for some reason...it offended.

Because you wanted to believe you fixed him.

You wanted to believe you were special.

But Violet King is the one he thinks is special.

"It's not fair," she shouted. "But nothing is fair. You don't have to pass on the unfairness, though, and you are. But you're the only one making that determination."

"She is what's right for the country. And therefore, I will continue on."

"You utter, heartless…"

"I told you I was."

"I might hate you," she said, the word coming out a whisper. "I truly might."

"And I'm sorry for that. I would rather you did not. But it does not mean I can make a different decision."

"You're the King, you could do whatever you want."

"Isn't that just the thing you were telling me I should not do?"

"Now you listen to me. Wonderful."

"She will learn to adjust."

But would Livia? Would she ever heal from this? From this devastation, not just of his marriage finally coming into the present, but knowing just how void of feeling he truly was.

She didn't think she could.

Except, it would be better, if that had cured her of loving him.

The sad thing was, it did not.

She broke the kiss, and stepped away from him. She had thought that memory might bring her some clarity, and it had.

She couldn't marry him.

But since nothing had done the job of eliminating her feelings for him, eliminating her desire for him…

Well, she would claim that.

"Take me back to the hotel," she whispered. Shame flooded her, heat flooding her face.

"Be very certain of what you're asking me," he said, his tone a warning.

"I'm certain," she said.

"Then let us go."

He wrapped his arm around her waist and led her from the dance floor. And when they arrived, she could see that their dessert had been wrapped up to go. And she felt sort of silly, how obvious things were, even to the waitstaff.

Except, she didn't care. Because she would not have to deal with the fallout of this. Because this was a goodbye, whether he knew it or not.

"I'm very certain," she said, not to him, but to herself.

And then he took her arm and led her out into the night.

CHAPTER SEVEN

FIRE STREAKED THROUGH his veins as they drove down the mountainside, heading toward Paris. But they would not be staying in the hotel that she had chosen. Rather, they would be going to his suite. Of course, he was in the same hotel that she was in. He wasn't a fool. He had not only known exactly where she was, he had availed himself to her room and he had her things moved into it. That should have been done the moment they had gone out to dinner. The staff had their orders, and of course they had complied.

He was a king, after all.

She wanted him.

And he was a little bit wary of how quickly she had changed her tune, that a bit of French bread and kissing had brought her to the place where she wanted to go to bed with him.

But he would not question his good fortune.

Livia was just a woman, like any other, and she was being given the chance to have money, power, a title. And because she was Livia, he did imagine that his reminding her she had a chance to do some very real good had brought her to this conclusion as well.

But still, she was human, his mouse.

He didn't know why that disappointed him slightly.

That she could be so easily convinced.

But then, there was also the chemistry between them.

Chemistry he had worked for years to deny. If it had become harder recently, he had done his best not to think of it. He had been promised to Violet, and while he would not claim to be a great man, he had intended to keep his vows to his American fiancée. Who had not kept hers, and had found herself in love with his brother.

She made no vows to you. You kidnapped her.

Technically, *Javier* had kidnapped her.

And Matteo had not been bothered. Not in the least. From the moment his brother had said that he and Violet were going to wed each other, Matteo had shifted focus.

It was his own fault after all, he had left Violet unattended with his brother.

And he had been away with Livia.

It had been a very important political summit.

And he could've brought Violet with him, but their connection was still very new, and she had been unhappy and he had a feeling that she would have only damaged any political outreach he was attempting, with her general bitterness at the state of things.

Fair enough.

So, it had been just him and Livia, who had been angry with him, frosty.

Since their fight when he had told her about Violet King.

"And when will you decide to speak to me again?"

"Not anytime soon," she huffed.

"You're putting on quite a brave face in the palace."

"Well, it's not good for morale for everyone to see what an ass I think you are."

"You forget yourself," he said, rolling his shoulders back and turning to walk the length of the hotel suite. Livia was sitting on the couch there, perched on the end, looking indignant, her shoulders rigid and straight, her legs crossed at the ankles. She looked everything good and proper, an admonishment of what she found improper in him.

"How good of you to think of morale. I have political alliances to make tonight, though, and it would not benefit me to have my assistant lurking in the background looking like she wants to stab me with one of the very tiny forks that we will find at this banquet."

"Why bother to have me lurking in the background?"

"You know I need you there."

"Oh. I see. So, you intend to keep me in the position I'm in even when you have a Queen?"

"All men keep their advisors when they marry."

"So she's simply decorative? Not your primary advisor?"

"No. She will not be my primary advisor. She's just a woman. From America. What does she know about politics? And, indeed, what does she know about Monte Blanco?"

"What's the point of it?"

"Optics." He shook his head. "Honestly, Livia, you are the one that taught me about such things. Told me how important it is. Shouldn't you be pleased?"

"I'm not pleased. I'm not pleased that you're acting like a marauding medieval barbarian."

"You are inconsistent." He stood in front of her expectantly.

"What?" she asked.

"My tie."

"You know how to tie your own tie."

"You do it better."

She looked up at him with furious eyes. She was wearing those big, gold spectacles she was so fond of. A strange choice, he had always thought. Exceedingly obvious, and not at all subtle. An announcement to the world, he supposed, that she was bookish. But she was beautiful, and those glasses couldn't hide it. Indeed, he found them quite charming, though he would never admit it to her.

He found her quite charming, even when she was furious, something else he would never admit to her.

"You're an ass," she repeated, her fingers moving resolutely over the black silk fabric of his tie.

"I'm not concerned about it."

"But then," she said, bristling, "you wouldn't be, would you? You're a beast."

"And yet, you remain."

"So I do. Call it a care for my country. Without me, we would be in true jeopardy."

"I see. So you see yourself as a rudder for our great nation."

"I steer the ship. To the best of my ability."

"And I'm the one who's arrogant."

"I never said I wasn't."

She disappeared, and emerged a moment later. Her hair was in a simple bun, and she wore very little makeup. She was wearing her typical uniform of black dress, though this one clung a bit more tightly to her curves. It was a dress that swept to the floor, flaring out like an unfurling lily as it fell past her knee.

It was not bright or obvious. She would not be quite so glittery as the other women in attendance.

But Livia always took pains not to set herself apart. He wouldn't have minded, as the years passed, if she made herself slightly more obviously a key player, rather than just waitstaff, but she never had. Had never shifted from the background to anything more.

She looked beautiful, though, he thought.

Perhaps it was her fury.

Nobody else dared challenge him in the way that she did. Only Javier ever did, and he was a prince.

It was the audacity of Livia that got to him.

It was expected for Javier to get angry with him sometimes. But not for his assistant.

It was a charming thing.

Charming.

Why was he feeling half so *charmed* by Livia at the moment? She was being a termagant.

"Let us away," she said.

They went downstairs, and a limo was waiting for them. Livia slid inside, her skirt fanning out around her, revealing a slit in the long, flowing black dress, showing off a length of pale leg.

Her legs were quite lovely. He had endeavored not to notice before.

He looked at her, and her profile, that staunch upturned nose, and the dramatic lips, her pert little chin.

The line of her neck, that curve at the back of it, was also quite something. She was a study in delicate lines, elegant swoops. She was soft. And yet… Not soft at all in her interaction.

"You're quite beautiful," he said.

She turned to him, and he found the anger that burned in her eyes was even more pronounced now than it had been a moment ago. "Are you trying to flatter me?"

"I don't do flattery. I thought you should know."

"Oh, yes, I do know, but I find that all of your behavior of late is quite a bit outside the character of the man I thought I knew."

"It was not a leading comment, simply a statement. You're beautiful, Livia."

Her cheeks turned pink, and she looked away from him. "How lucky for me."

"I imagine no matter that you dressed in black men pay quite a bit of attention to you at these events."

"It wouldn't matter if they did. I'm working."

"Ah yes, always working, aren't you?"

"Yes. As my boss, *you* should know *that*."

When they got out of the car, he took her arm.

"What are you doing?"

"I wish you to stay with me tonight."

"I don't stay with you at these sorts of things, as well you know. We do not come in together. I go through the back."

"You're not going through the back tonight," he said, his voice hard. "You must endeavor to find a way to deal with that."

"This was not the plan."

"And I decide what the plans are. You may organize them, but I have the ultimate decision-making power. I suggest you find a way to cope with that."

"Inconvenient…"

But the beginning of her tirade was cut off by the fact that they had arrived at the entrance to the Grand Hotel. And then, she was far too good at her job to do anything but smile. As he had known that she would be. It was how Livia was.

The perfect assistant, the perfect advisor. She always had been.

In fact, it was difficult for him to recall how he had ever gotten along without her. He didn't like to think of it, not really. For she was the perfect partner in every way, and that was undeniable.

Even when she was angry with him.

She nearly vibrated with it now, but she kept it to herself.

"Just like you taught me," he whispered in her ear.

She turned her head, her face a scant inch from his. "What?"

"Smiling. Even when you don't feel like it."

She scrunched her nose up, and he could tell that it was a fury that contorted her expression thus, but also that no one else would recognize it.

No, all they would see was a small, beautiful woman, looking up at him.

"Careful," he said. "They might think that you're gazing adoringly at me."

She nearly hissed. "I'm not."

"I'm only telling you, optics."

"You and your damn optics."

"They're *your* damn optics, of a technicality."

They swept into the ballroom together, where he was announced, as was fitting his station. But of course, they did not announce Livia.

He could see the person making the introductions was quite put off by the fact that he had shown up with someone unexpected.

But whether anybody there knew it or not, Livia was not unexpected.

Livia was with him wherever he went.

He wondered why he had never brought her in with him like this before.

You know why.

Because it didn't matter that she worked for him, and nothing more. People would assume, of course, that she was more to him than that.

In point of fact, she was.

"I'm very sorry." A man came from the recesses of the room, melting into the floor in a suit that announced him as staff, rather than one of the dignitaries in attendance. "But Your Majesty, we did not know you would be bringing a guest with you. And we did not set the table as such."

"Then I suggest you remedy that."

"Yes, sir."

"And why is it you feel you must come to me with your concerns. Surely you can speak to someone else, and make it appear as if you magically did your jobs without having to apologize in such an obsequious fashion."

"Stop it," Livia said, in full view of the man. "You're being a terror."

The man's lips twitched, as he fought to keep his expression neutral.

"Perhaps I would like the lady to sit on the floor."

"That will make a wonderful headline."

"I will see to getting her place sitting right away."

"What is the matter with you?" Livia rounded on him.

"I might ask you the same question, as you have been acting the part of guttersnipe since…"

"Since you kidnapped Violet King and brought her to the palace? I don't approve. Was that not clear?"

"You don't approve. Yet all you do is move palely around the palace, looking for all to see like a serene handmaiden."

"I am nobody's handmaiden, as you well know. And you want me to yell at you in front of everyone else?"

"You seem on the verge of doing it here."

"Because I'm appalled at you. Shocked and appalled."

"So appalled," he said, moving his arm from her elbow, to her lower back. And she went stiff.

Her body was supple. It really was quite lovely.

Lust tightened low in his stomach and he castigated himself.

Even attempting to cause her grief—as he was at the moment—he did not want to feel these things for Livia.

He had always been aware of what he must not do with her. Of what he must not feel.

His age, his position, her dependence on him…

It was all impossible. And what sort of impossible situation would it become if he carried on an affair with Livia while married to Violet? Though, granted, many men might find it convenient to have his mistress and wife housed in the same place.

But it was a recipe for disaster. And Livia would never quietly be a mistress.

She would likely crusade about, joining forces with Violet. Unionizing. That was all he needed.

Anyway, Livia had never evinced the slightest bit of interest in him in that way. She was nothing but brisk and efficient, and a woman who wanted him would scarcely yell at him and all other things that Livia did to him on a daily basis.

She did not conduct herself as a woman who wanted sexual attention from him.

He did not have the words for what that made him feel.

He could not have her preoccupied with such things if he expected her to do her job. That much was true. But…

A spark smoldered in his blood when he looked at her for too long.

And he was not accustomed to being near a woman who did not react to him as a potential partner. He did not know if he wanted it from her, or not. And it was the not knowing that frustrated as much as it intrigued.

"I suggest you get your emotions in order," he said. "For I am at the end of my patience. This is a very important event. We have inroads that we have to make at this summit tomorrow. And it begins tonight. You know how it is. I need you with me. I cannot do it without you."

"Why don't you think you can do it without me? You've been doing all of this just fine with me in the background for years."

"I know everything there is to know about the economy of Monte Blanco, I know everything that I must to make this alliance work. But I do not know how to do...diplomacy."

"You are much better at it than you used to be."

"But I need you there. I need you to help. And I need you to not be opposing me at every turn."

"You are difficult," she said.

"And so are you. It is what I like about you, and I assume on a good day, it is what you like about me."

"Who said I like you?" she said, looking up at him from beneath her lashes. "You sign my paychecks."

A harsh statement, and he was surprised at the

note of discomfort it left in his gut. For he did not care about things like that, like whether someone liked him. Least of all Livia. It had never occurred to him that she might not. For were they not, in many ways, two halves of one whole?

"You like me," he said.

But they didn't get a chance to continue their banter because the tables were set and they were ushered to them.

He had never had the chance to see Livia in quite this environment. And he was stunned by how easy it seemed for her. She was able to carry on conversations seamlessly. He introduced her as his advisor, and it was accepted that she was so. Her opinion given weight, just as he imagined it should be.

And as he watched her speak, as he watched her bring everyone at the table onto her side, he realized that she was so much more than he had ever given her credit for.

She should be promoted. Not just be an assistant or an advisor. Perhaps some sort of liaison. She was the diplomat; she knew everything about politics and Monte Blanco. Everything about the country itself.

He could remember her as she'd been. Skinny and tragic and bedraggled when he had first found her. And she was as far away from that now as a woman born to be queen might be.

Queen.

The talks the table continued for long hours, while

other revelers that were not diplomats of one country or another enjoyed dancing, and desserts.

"Shall we take this conversation to the balcony?"

One of the representatives from the United States asked that question, and Livia nodded eagerly. "Yes. I would be happy to continue the conversation outside."

"And you, Your Majesty?"

"Of course. If we have exhausted the table's goodwill for the topic."

"I fear very much we might have," the man said, laughing.

One of the leaders from the United Kingdom joined them, and they stood out there talking for many hours, about the ways in which each country could benefit the other. And he felt, by the end, that when they convened tomorrow for the actual summit, things would go well.

The diplomat from the United States left first, followed by the man from the United Kingdom.

And that left himself and Livia standing there out on the balcony. She wrapped her arms around herself, rubbing her pale arms. "I'm sorry about our fight earlier," she said. "It was pointless. You're right. This is what matters. Monte Blanco. And this went… Well. It went well."

"I would like to think so."

"I do feel sorry for Violet."

"I don't. She will be treated well."

"But without freedom."

He leaned against the balustrade that overlooked the grand gardens below. "Do any of us have true freedom, Livia?"

The words scraped raw against his throat and he disliked how deep a place they came from.

"I don't know how to answer that." Her tone was carefully bland. And it angered him. She had been charming inside, and here she was so careful with him.

She was like that sometimes. Fire and unguarded in a moment, and then unreachable in another and he hated it. Because he could not figure out why. And he could not force her to change when she had her mind set on retreating as she had now.

"Think about it," he pushed. "We are all born into a certain position. And then life does what it will with us. Those who have control of us when we are children… They get to have so much control over what we become. As we discussed with my father… He may not have been able to determine what manner of king I am, but his hooks are in me that I have not been able to successfully remove. I still have nightmares."

Those nightmares she alone had seen. She had touched him then, without fear. Without a wall.

There was silence for a moment.

"So do I," she said softly.

The catch in her voice betrayed her. She was letting her guard down and he found he wanted that.

He felt, for some strange reason, like there was sand running through an hourglass. That if they did not have this moment, they would never have it.

Because of Violet? Perhaps.

Whatever the reason, he felt they had to speak like this now, or they never would.

It mattered, just then.

"Because of decisions your mother made. Because you were put out on the streets. Violet King has had a comparably easy life, at least as far as I'm aware. She has money, and influence. And now... Her father has made a decision that is impacting her. How is she any different from us? Except I will not be cruel to her."

"What if she wished to fall in love? To have her husband love her back?"

Those words made it feel like an avalanche had gone off inside him.

"Then she will be disappointed. But as disappointments go..." He looked at her, at her elegant profile. She seemed so solitary, his mouse. Right next to him and yet...very far away. "Did you ever expect to be loved, Livia?"

The only sound in the air now was the crickets, chirping from the garden below. She did not move. Did not look at him. "No. I didn't expect to be loved.

Not even for one moment of my life. The greatest thing I could hope for was to live."

She looked at him then, her eyes brighter than stars.

"And have your expectations been surpassed now?" he asked, his voice that of a stranger's.

She nodded. "Yes. I must confess they have. For this has been better than any scenario I could have ever imagined for myself. I cannot pretend otherwise."

He ground his teeth together. "I never imagined I would be loved. I imagined having loyalty given to me by the people of my country. I imagined... Not in my wildest dreams did I imagine love."

"But perhaps she did."

The soft rebuke should have wounded him, and yet it wasn't feelings for Violet he had in this moment. But his soft, strong Livia....

Should she not expect more than mere survival?

"And Violet will overcome the disappointment, for there are many other things in life that are vastly more important."

"Yes, I suppose that is so."

"It will not be so bad for her. No doubt her business will increase tenfold, and from everything I've seen about her, her business is her life. As far as I'm aware she's never had a relationship. All my surveillance points to the fact that the growth of her company is her one true love. And I believe that her goals will mesh nicely with mine."

The silence between them filled with night air

and crickets as they stood, saying nothing for a long while.

Then Livia spoke. Her voice puncturing his chest like a knife in the dark.

"What do you think it would be like?"

"What?"

"To be in love."

Such a simple question, and one everything in him turned away from.

"That sort of thing is the opiate of the masses, I fear. Nothing real about it. Nothing substantial."

"You don't think?"

He looked at her. "Have you ever seen it?"

She shook her head. "No. Sadly. My father was never around. I'm not even entirely certain who he was. But he did not love my mother. I do not even know where he was from or what he did. But there was no love there, clearly, or she would have spoken of him. And I thought she loved me, but it turned out not to be. And you…"

"My father saw me as a plaything." The words were hard and harsh. "Whether or not it was as an exorcism for his psychopathy, or a true belief inside of himself that he was training me to be a hardened leader, I don't know. But he seemed to enjoy hurting me. Javier and I have a loyalty between ourselves."

"And that's all?"

A muscle in his face ticked. "I would wish better for him," Matteo said. "Better for him than to be me."

"Do you think you'll find better?"

"I don't know." He hated that. Not knowing. This entire moment was full of not knowing.

"You *do* think there's better. Is it love, do you think, that makes the difference?"

"Perhaps."

"So you acknowledge that… That if it is real… It might be wonderful?"

"A great many things could be classified that way. It would not change the way things are." He gripped the railing. Hard. "I hope you find someone who loves you, Mouse."

She looked up at him, her eyes wide. Startled.

"Why?"

He moved toward her, suddenly compelled by her pale silhouette. "Because you've seen enough hardship, I think. Enough hardship to last you a lifetime."

The air seemed to disappear entirely.

"I certainly think so," she said, sounding breathless. "But why don't you want better for yourself?"

"Better for me is simply not being my father." It felt like the stone of the building behind him was sitting on his shoulders. For Livia assumed this was a simple task, and he feared it was not. To hate his father would make it simple. The reality… The reality was much more complicated. "And I'll take that. Unhappily. It does not grieve me if the future set before me is only as lofty as that."

"And me?"

He reached out, and did something he thought he might regret. He touched her face, and found it soft. Let his hand move down to her chin. She took a sharp, indrawn breath, but she didn't move away.

"You are the most singular creature I have ever known. Even when you're being a harpy. In fact, perhaps especially then, because nobody dares challenge me the way that you do. You have fought diligently for our country tonight. You... You among all people deserve love, if such a thing exists."

"Even the façade of it?"

"People seem quite happy."

"Some of them do, yes."

"But you can never leave me," he said. "Whatever man catches your eye, you must stay with me."

"I don't think I could." She turned away from him.

"Why not?"

"I cannot be yours while professing to be someone else's, surely you must know that."

"Well, if he is from Monte Blanco, I don't think you will see a problem with it. I'm the King. So everything is mine first."

"Thank you for reminding me," she said, nearly laughing. "That even when you're being kind, you're still you. And still arrogant underneath it all."

"And you are still a feral little creature. Even underneath all that sophistication you put on."

"A compliment."

"And I take your insult such as well."

"Matteo…"

"Yes?"

But she turned away. And so he reached out, and gripped her chin again, leaning down as he turned her face up, bringing their mouths within a whisper of each other. And then, everything stopped. Time was suspended.

And held.

He had been on the verge of kisses before. Though typically, he just took them, and the women he was with claimed them right back. No pausing. No hesitation.

This was not a hesitation.

It was a profound discovery. And he could do nothing but sit there in it. In this realization that what he wanted more than anything, right in that moment, was to taste her.

To taste her vile temper, her recriminations, her compliments. To drink them all in and somehow take them inside of himself. So that he could feel all that she did. That fire and passion. For he had just thought to himself how she was his other half in many ways. And this was the half that he yearned for. The one that contained all that bright, brilliant emotion that his body nearly refused to let him have. Pain, he had that. Anger, aplenty. But the rest… She contained all of that. A great mystery, a great certainty.

"Livia," he whispered.

"You will marry Violet King?" she asked, her voice sounding almost like she was drunk.

"Yes," he said.

She moved away from him. "Don't do that to me again."

"What did I..."

"Just don't. Tonight's been strange, and not at all like what we normally are. Let us not repeat it."

And then she turned and walked back into the ballroom.

They were at the hotel, and he pulled her out of the car and into his arms on the street. And he kissed her. With all the longing he had felt in that moment at the hotel in Spain. That deep desire to be with her. He had held himself back then because she had asked him to.

Because...

Because he had been resolute in his course then, and he could see now that it had been the wrong one.

What was it about Livia that always made him have to confront his flaws? He preferred to labor under the assumption he had none. That by excising his heart, he had done away with the potential for mistakes. But she was ever a reminder that he was human.

And now he reveled in it.

For only a human, only a man, could enjoy the feel of a woman in his arms quite this way.

And he kissed her, right there on the streets for anyone to see. Claiming.

Because she was his.

From the moment he had taken her off the streets, she had been his.

She had tried to run from it, from him, but they were inevitable.

He could see that now. That night he had brought her to the gala, it had been a trial, for her being his Queen. It was as if something in him had known it before his mind had, and he had never experienced anything quite like that. But in many ways, it was like that thing inside him had known it from the moment he'd seen her out on the street. That she was to be taken in, for just this moment. That her destiny was to be the Queen of Monte Blanco. The country needed her. He was absolutely convinced of that now. She had been guiding him all this time, had been advising him and organizing him, and he could see now that the common bond—other than himself—when it came to all the growth in the country and the growth in himself, was Livia.

She was inevitable.

As was this.

Fate, if you believed in such things.

He did not. But how could he deny that there was something of a higher power at work here? It didn't matter. Because he was not in a position to deny it, nor did he want to. Tonight, he just wanted her.

When he could drag his mouth away from hers, he led her into the hotel, bringing her into the private elevator that took him to the top floor, to his suite.

His thumbprint allowed the doors to open, bringing them out to the luxury penthouse.

"I…" She sounded dizzy.

"Did you not realize we were not headed to your room?"

"I can't say that I noticed much of anything."

"I had us moved."

Her eyes flickered, and he had a feeling he was about to get a lecture on his arrogance again, so he silenced her with a kiss. And drunk her in deep. He could taste the notes of the wine she had at dinner, could taste the sun somehow, and something that was essentially her.

And he knew that there was no turning back now.

CHAPTER EIGHT

LIVIA WAS DIZZY with desire. The way that he held her, the way that he kissed her. She couldn't even bring herself to be angry at the high-handedness inherent in him moving all of her things into this beautiful penthouse. She had seen a great many spectacular hotel rooms, suites and apartments over the years. Had been living in a palace for nearly a decade. But still, she was never immune to the luxury around her. Because she could never forget to be grateful for comfort when she had been so uncomfortable for so long.

But this was all somehow different. Because it wasn't comfort in the way she understood it. There was a lushness to it, almost a sensuality. As if every texture in the room called out an invitation to sex, every surface a potential place for her to spend her desire for him.

She was not naïve.

She had known what sex was for a long time.

Her people were earthy. And then on top of that, she had spent so much time on the street she had seen any number of women selling themselves to buying men. She had been groped and harassed and chased down by those seeking the same thing from her. Had been accosted by men in suits offering money in exchange for lewd acts. And while she had managed to escape any personal experience, she knew about sex. Both the violence that could come with it, and the pleasure.

Of course, knowing about and being prepared to experience were two very different things. But she was about to. With him.

It had always had to be this way.

He would have to be the first.

Because if she didn't know what it was to be with Matteo, then she would never be with anybody.

It just wouldn't happen.

Because he had formed her every thought about attraction, so he would have to be the one to introduce her to the pleasures of the flesh.

But all of her justifications went out the window when his mouth moved over hers.

And then, he kissed her neck, moved down to her collarbone, pushing the spaghetti strap of her dress off of her shoulder. And then the other. Her bodice fell, and her breasts were exposed. They were not particularly large. But then, they weren't small either. Just sort of unremarkable, she thought.

Everyday breasts.

But he let out a sound, a growl, that reverberated inside of her, and seemed to suggest something entirely different.

"You are beautiful," he said, his voice rough.

And it echoed that night three weeks ago, when he'd said that to her for the first time, in the limousine, before they went into the hotel.

"Do you really think so?"

"I do," he said, looking at her. "You know how hard I fought to keep myself from ever… It would have been a grave sin against you, Livia."

"Tell me," she said, suddenly desperate. "Tell me how long you thought I was beautiful."

"It is a shame to me," he said.

"But it is water in a desert to me."

"Very well." He growled, lifting her up off the ground, and she let out an undignified squeak. Then he put his hand on one of her breasts, drawing his thumb slowly over her nipple, his gaze filled with intent concentration as he watched himself touch her. "I remember the night I first asked you to be my assistant. And you were wearing red. I do not know why."

"It was my birthday," she whispered.

"How foolish of me." He put his hand on her face, his eyes intense. "To not remember that. But I do remember your dress. I thought you beautiful. And impossibly young. So…vulnerable."

"I had stabbed men by then. I was hardly vulnerable."

"And then when I would catch you examining the tiles in the ballroom, as if you were looking for any speck of dirt there that might defy you."

"Why would you know something like that?"

"Because of the way your brow would increase when you concentrated. And I thought you beautiful."

"Oh."

"Then there was the night you came into my room, and I was naked. You brought me a drink and you sat with me. And it was tenderness in a way I had never known. And I thought you beautiful."

She closed her eyes and fought against the tears that were threatening to build.

"Then, you yelled at me in a wild fury in my office when I told you about Violet. You were in a rage like I had never seen you. And I thought you beautiful. Like when I taught you to dance in my office and you looked up to me with trust and openness and let me hold you in my arms even though you and I both know the cost of trusting another person that way. And I thought you beautiful."

"Matteo…"

"So you see, this is not new. It is only that I said it for the first time recently. Not that I thought it for the first time."

"Make love to me."

"That's what I'm already doing, *querida*."

"Don't call me that."

"Mouse," he whispered. "But you must admit, it is not sexy."

"But it's mine."

And that was the end of that, for he kissed her again, his hand still playing havoc on her breast, causing showers of sparks to bounce around inside her stomach. Then he took his mouth away from hers, and moved down to her breast, taking one nipple and sucking it deep. She arched in his arms, the desperate need building between her legs undeniable.

Unstoppable.

He moved his mouth to her other breast, and she felt like she might die. He strode across the room then, depositing her on the center of the very large bed. And then he moved away from her, standing at the foot of it.

"Matteo," she said, not caring if she sounded as if she was begging. She would beg him. She would beg him for more, for his touch, for his possession. Anything, so that he wouldn't stop.

But then, his hands moved to his shirt, and he began to unbutton it deftly, dropping it and the suit jacket down to the floor and leaving him bare chested. Oh, she had seen his chest many times, and it always thrilled her. But this still felt like the first time. The first time seeing that broad, muscular chest covered with just the right amount of dark hair. Those perfect ab muscles, and the deep cut right at his hip bones.

Because now, she would actually get to touch him. Now, he was not just an unobtainable symbol, wandering around in front of her as if she wasn't there, the ultimate sign of her sexlessness, that he didn't even bother to dress completely to meet with her.

No. He had said he thought her beautiful. And he was there, half-naked and ready for her.

And she found she could not keep still. She launched herself to the edge of the bed and put her hands on his chest.

She was touching him. Finally. She had seen him up close over the years, but he might as well have been behind a wall of glass. Because that was how unavailable he was to her. Looking, but never touching. And she had been so certain that she never would.

But finally, finally she was able to put her hands on him. Matteo.

She nearly wept with it, but he kissed her again, swallowing the sob even as it rose up in her throat.

She kissed him, letting her hands explore his chest, his stomach, luxuriating in the feel of his muscles, of the body hair, the heat of his skin. He was such a man. The masculine to her feminine. Hard and beautiful and unparalleled. He was everything she had ever fantasized about, and more. He was a revelation in the form of a human. For Livia felt beautiful in his arms. Felt spectacular and unique, and nothing like the poor, sad abandoned creature she had felt like for most of her days.

Because nothing could really erase that. Not the success that she had found working at the palace, not the many intervening years. It wasn't so simple to just erase those years spent alone.

That abandonment. That trauma.

No, it would never be quite so simple. But right now, at least, she could feel something like healed. Something special, held in his arms.

He laid her down onto the bed, coming over her, a commanding warrior that made her shiver beneath his fierce gaze. She had always known that he was dangerous and had taken a great sort of satisfaction in knowing so. That she was protected by a man who was, at his core, dangerous.

But now he was hers to touch, hers to kiss. Now she could make him shudder with desire, and did, as she nipped his lower lip while he continued a bold exploration of her body. He pushed her red dress down, past her waist, her hips, drawing it completely off of her, then turning his focus to the waistband of her panties. He teased the delicate skin just beneath and she shivered. She couldn't have fathomed that it would be like this. That he would be like this. At least, not for her. All of the women she had to get parting gifts for, who had left his bed, had been very, very sad their association had ended, and now she could see why.

For he wove delicious torture wherever he touched, left behind burn marks on her skin with the heat of his hands. And then, he allowed his fingers to inch slowly beneath that flimsy fabric, finding her center between her thighs, finding her wet and ready and filled with desire for him. He stroked her there, the pleasure that she found white-hot and brilliant. She could feel the muscles in her thighs quaking as he stroked her, long and slow, drawing circles over the most sensitive part of her. She shifted, arching her hip, and he pressed a finger deep inside of her. She cried out at the unfamiliar invasion, but then nearly wept for the beauty of it. Matteo was inside of her. And it was brilliant. And there would be more.

So much more.

And this might be it. Her last night with him. Her first night with him. But she would pour everything into this. And she would hold nothing back. Because she would be broken by leaving him. Whether they had this or not. So she would seize this fantasy for the girl who had slept on cold streets. Who had held herself while she cried. For the girl who had loved a king knowing she could never have him. Who had cried herself to sleep when he told her about his engagement to another woman.

For *that* girl, she would have this pleasure.

Have this connectedness. She kissed him, reveling in the pleasure he created between them. And she let her hands roam over his body, let them move to the front of his slacks, as she undid the closure there, felt the hardness pressing insistently against her. He wanted her.

He really did. So regardless of whether or not he had asked her to be his Queen because of convenience, she could know that. That he was attracted to her. That he wanted this. His body could not lie about it. Which was good, because her own could not either. Because that slickness between her legs advertised her need for him, and as he added a second finger, she gasped, rocking against him, desperately seeking fulfillment. But she wouldn't be fulfilled. Not until she had him. All of him.

With fumbling fingers, she tried to get his slacks pushed off completely, but he had to assist, pressing his body against hers, completely naked, chest to chest, thigh to thigh. His skin was so hot. And his desire was pushing against her with ferocity.

In this moment, she was wanted. Gloriously and without boundaries. And she would take it. More than take it. She would use it to rebuild. Use it to create something new. For she would know what it was. And there was some deep, undeniable satisfaction buried in the truth that he wanted something from her she wasn't going to give.

That she would maybe be the one to leave him wanting more. And perhaps that was revenge against her mother more than it was anything, perhaps it had nothing to do with Matteo at all. But she had spent nine years wanting the man, so maybe it did.

A small, petty revenge that came with blindingly brilliant pleasure. She would take it.

He growled, kissing her, and then she could think of nothing more, as his fingers worked in and out of her body, as his lips played havoc with her. And then, he began to kiss his way down her body, blazing a trail past her belly button, down to the very heart of her, where he teased and stroked her with his fingers even as he consumed her with his mouth.

She gasped, rocking and rolling her hips, her head thrashing back and forth on the pillow as he brought her to new heights of pleasure she hadn't known were possible. And then, she shattered, broke into a million pieces of crystalline glass, and she had no idea how he still held on to her, how he still pushed her higher, farther, with his wicked lips and tongue, because she didn't think she was rooted to the earth anymore.

She was scattered in the wind.

She was all the glitter that she'd contained inside of herself. And she couldn't be distinguished from it.

Not anymore.

While she was still sobbing and gasping her pleasure, he rose up over her body and kissed her, the flavor of her own desire heady on his lips as he pressed himself against the entrance to her body.

And then he thrust home.

She cried out in pain, and he stilled, holding her

tightly against him, making a low, whispering sound, as if he was quieting a frightened creature.

And she quieted. She felt the pain between her thighs begin to ease, felt her body begin to relax around him.

And it didn't take long for pleasure to begin to build again.

He moved back out slowly, then pushed back inside, and she moaned. And he took that as his signal that he could move.

And so he did. Establishing a rhythm, as he had done in his office when he had taught her to dance. She could almost feel it, echoing in her chest, in her soul.

One, two, three, four.

One, two, three, four.

It was a different sort of rhythm, but it lived inside her all the same. It rose up like a wave, wrapping itself around her, that rhythm, that sound, simply in her blood.

And it all made sense then, why she had been able to dance with him that way. Because it was always meant to be like this. Always. And impossibly, she felt another climax building inside of her, and she didn't think she could handle it. Honestly, thought it might destroy her.

But he held her tight. "Let go," he growled.

"Yes," she whispered, grabbing hold of his face and meeting his gaze.

Her lion. So fierce and powerful. But with a thorn in his paw.

He had said she had removed it, but she had not gotten to the one in his heart. She didn't think anyone could. Not even his mouse.

It was a terrible sorrow, but it was eclipsed by the desire that rioted through her like a storm. And then, she broke again, a horse cry of desire rising in her throat even as her internal muscles contracted around him, deep inside.

And then, he let go.

He spilled himself inside of her on a growl, his release making him pulse, making him tremble. And right then, she felt they were equals.

No longer the king and the street urchin. But two people unraveled, undone. Broken by desire and pleasure. Brought down to nothing but needed.

And need they had found sated only in each other.

And as she lay there against the mattress, breathing hard, her heart beating erratically, she felt that same rush of joy she had felt when he told her he wasn't going to marry Violet. When all seemed possible and new.

And it did. Like the sky had opened up. Right there over the bed.

"Apparently, Violet has fallen in love with Javier."

Livia looked up from her computer. "He… She… *What?*"

"While we were gone, it turns out. While we were handling that big important alliance for Monte Blanco, my brother was stealing my bride."

"You don't seem upset." She narrowed her eyes and examined him.

"I'm not. It is what I wanted for him, after all. I wanted him to find love, I just didn't assume it would be with my fiancée. But I suppose all's well that ends well. Monte Blanco could still have the benefit of Violet's influence, and she and Javier can be happy. And not even you can be angry at me anymore, Mouse."

"I think I'll find some new reasons," she said absently.

She sat there for a moment, her heart buoyant in her chest.

And suddenly, it felt like it might have burst open. He wasn't marrying Violet. She was going to marry Javier. She…

"Will you excuse me for a moment?"

"Certainly."

She left the office, and ducked into the nearest alcove of the palace, leaning against the stone wall and pressing her hand to her breast. "He's not marrying her."

She wanted to shout. She wanted to cry. For everything that had transpired on the trip had been… She had never felt like Matteo might have noticed her in that way, but during this trip she had. The way he had held her chin, the way he had looked at her...

Her foolish heart had begun to dream, and now... now he wasn't even engaged and he...

Then the cold hard dagger of reality stabbed into her.

He had seen how she was with diplomats on the trip. He had been impressed with her. And he had re-iterated just how important she was to him. How he didn't want her to leave him even if she were to marry someone else. And she knew Matteo. Knew that his arrogance far surpassed just about anything else, and what he wanted, he went out and got.

Matteo was going to propose to *her*.

He would wait. He would wait until Javier and Violet had married. Until there had been a suitable lapse in time so that it was clear that he had not be-trayed his fiancée in any way. And then he would... He would ask her to be his wife. No, he would de-mand it. Because that's who he was. It would never occur to him that she would say no. Not because he thought she was in love with him—thank God for that—but because he would simply assume that what he was asking was so logical no one would deny him. And immediately, her heart crumpled with pain.

She didn't know what to do. The reality of the situation was that things had changed. He was the same man. It didn't matter that the circumstances had shifted. He hadn't. He wouldn't. He was King Matteo of Monte Blanco, a man who considered possession of emotions to be a near crime as far as his own heart was concerned. That wouldn't change just because his circumstances with Violet King had changed. And she could see the path that he would take, and the reason he would get on it. She could see that he would choose her as a logical course of action, and it would be worse…

It would be worse than watching him marry someone else.

Because if she had to stand back and watch him marry Violet, then she would've had to watch that other woman be consigned to a life without love. And she wouldn't have envied her half so much as she might have otherwise. That would've been bearable. In a strange, small, twisted way, she found that she would have been able to bear that.

But she couldn't bear it for herself. She couldn't bear a life without love.

Not loving him the way that she did. If she hadn't loved him, it would be an entirely different story. If she hadn't felt the way that she did for him, cutting down deep into her soul, then it wouldn't be so painful. So impossible. But she did, and it was.

And she knew what it was like.

When someone else could drop you off callously, leave you standing there, alone and frightened and confused, with nothing but a sugary sweet to comfort you. Yes, she knew what that was like. She had endured it once, and she refused to put herself through it again. She refused to ever expose herself to such pain ever again.

Not for him. Not for anyone.

Not for king. Not for country.

And so she would have to steel herself. Because when he asked, she would have to say no. She would have to show no emotion whatsoever. She would have to tell herself every single day that he could walk into the office and propose marriage, any day. At any moment.

So that when he finally did, she reacted not at all. Didn't even bat an eyelash. It would destroy her. It would be as a knife, cutting across the vulnerable places in her soul.

But she would do it.

And then, she would offer to find him another wife. Because it was the only way. It was the only way she would be able to cope with all of this. The only way she would be able to be strong. Resolute in herself.

There was no other choice. *There was no other choice.*

She couldn't forget.

She could not afford to let emotion take over.

He never would.

And that was what she had to remember.

The joy that she felt inside of her chest deflated.

This was no different than that moment he told

her that his engagement was off. Yes, everything bright and beautiful seemed possible for a moment. But only for a moment. Because reality remained. He was no different, and neither was she.

She got out of bed, her heart hammering.

"We will go back to Monte Blanco," he said, sitting up, the sheets sliding down and only barely covering any part of him.

"We will not," she said, panic rioting through her now.

"There is no discussion to be had," he said, frowning. "You are to be my bride, Livia."

"No. I didn't say that."

"You said that you wanted me."

"I did. And I had you. It was lovely, don't get me wrong. But… This was not an agreement to be your wife."

"The hell it wasn't."

"Do you marry every woman you have sex with, Matteo? Only, we both know you don't, as I have been responsible for shoving a great many of them out of your life. So what exactly did you think I would do when you proposed to me?"

"I thought you would say yes. Because I thought you had a brain in your head."

"I have spent years seeing the way that you treat women. As disposable, easily discarded things."

"That isn't fair," he said. "The women that I've been in relationships with have known full well how it was going to end. Quickly. They knew that I would offer a good time in bed, and a few hours of conversation. Civilized conversation. They knew that there would be nothing more than that. And they knew it from the beginning. I have never gone about being a breaker of hearts. No one has ever had their hearts engaged. Do not pretend now that you are responding to something you imagined."

"No. You're misconstruing what I'm saying. I have watched you have feelings for no one. Why would I consent to live with such a man? And what will happen when you tire of me? When you get bored? You will simply find yourself another lover, because your emotions are otherwise engaged. Or rather, not engaged at all."

"I will not. I will honor our vows."

"No. I'm not a fool. And you thought that I would be so grateful for your attentions that I would simply fall down onto my knees and accept. You thought that you could come in making demands and that I would comply. Because you thought that I was small and desperate. You can say whatever you want about why you call me Mouse, but I don't believe you. I think it is because you find me small and grateful, and you thought that I would still be that same desperate, grasping creature that you found on the streets. Oh, that I should be so lucky as to gain your attentions. As to be offered this elevation as your Queen. But no. I will not take it, and I do not want it."

"It is too late," he said.

"What do you mean?"

"It is too late for you to refuse. You made love with me."

"A commonplace act for *you*."

"But not for you," he ground out. "As it became abundantly clear when we joined."

"Are you truly shocked that I was a virgin? When would I have had the time to have a lover?"

"You have plenty of your own life, Mouse. If I had time for sex, I assumed you did as well."

She could tell by his tone the revelation truly stunned him but she couldn't fathom why. Or why he cared.

And in this moment she didn't much care. He was infuriating her.

"You know that isn't true. Because everything in your life is made easier by the actions conducted in mine. I am busy, while you are abed with any number of models."

"That isn't true. You paint a picture to appease the anger that you feel now, when you're simply indignant because you gave in. You can deny it all you want, and you can act ruffled of feather, but you wanted this, and you wanted me. Now you know it can't be hidden, and you're upset. Because you've been exposed. But your discomfort is not my concern. And you are coming back to Monte Blanco with me."

"I will not." She shimmied, slipping the dress back on. "I'm going back to my room."

"You don't have a room anymore," he said, his voice hard. "You are staying here. With me."

"I'm not. I'm leaving. I'll go back to my apartment, then."

"No."

"You cannot tell me what to do."

He picked her up off of the ground, handily holding her over his shoulder as he hunted around on the floor for pants. Somehow, he managed to hold her and put them on.

"You're coming with me. You are mine now, end of story."

"You…" She wiggled. "You have no authority to do this."

"Watch me."

"It's kidnap," she said.

"Oh, well."

"How dare you?"

"With surprising ease."

And then he walked into the elevator of the suite, completely shirtless, carrying her over his shoulder. It was late, and there was no one down in the lobby of the hotel other than an employee. Who didn't even look at them.

"You can't do this," she reiterated, hoping to get a response out of the employee, who only looked the other way. "This is outrageous."

"So it is."

"Put me down," she demanded.

She looked over her shoulder, trying to get a view of his face.

"No," he said, simply, and with no inflection.

"I said put me down."

"No," he repeated.

And suddenly she realized that he was echoing his proposal and her refusal of last week.

"Matteo…"

"I have told you from the beginning, Mouse, that a monster lived inside of me. That I was capable of all manner of things. And you told me… What did you tell me? That it wasn't true? That I had no need to be so vigilant? That I was not my father? Let us test the limits of that, then. And your trust in me. All that you think I am capable of, and that what you think I am not. Let us plumb the depths of it, shall we?"

He bundled her into the sports car, and she was trying to gain her balance when he started the engine and began to pull away from the curb.

"You are…unbelievable," she said as he whizzed through the city streets, heading to God knew where.

"I am the King," he said. "I will have that which is mine."

CHAPTER NINE

AN HOUR LATER he sat on his private plane with an angry Livia sitting across from him. Her dress was bunched up around her knees, which were pulled up against her chest, her mouth turned down into a sulky frown. Her hair was disheveled, absolutely wrecked from their lovemaking earlier. She had thought she would leave him? Incomprehensible. Inconceivable.

He had taken her virginity.

He had done what he had vowed never to do to her, without the offer of marriage.

With marriage on the table, it was acceptable. Without it was not. It was that simple. He could not—*ever*—leave her to take another lover. The very idea sent him into a black rage. So she was coming back with him.

And kidnap is somehow acceptable?

It was not stealing if the item belongs to you. Livia belonged to him. It was clear enough in his mind.

Something fierce burned in his chest and he did not wish to guess at what it might be.

It didn't matter.

He was set on his course. He would deal with the fallout later. Once they were back in Monte Blanco, everything would be simpler. She would not be allowed to leave. Things were more complicated when she had been in another country. A place where he did not have ultimate domain. But he did in Monte Blanco, and he would exercise it.

All would be well.

"Would you like a drink?" he asked, standing up and making his way over to the bar in the corner of the living area of the large, spacious cabin.

"I would not," she said.

"A good idea, though perhaps a bit premature. You could be carrying my child."

He had not used protection. And Livia had been a virgin, so he assumed there was a possibility that she could be pregnant.

Or on her way to pregnant, as the case may be.

"Oh," she said, the sound filled with distress.

"Things you did not consider when you thought you might walk away from me."

"I didn't think of it."

"Of course not. You lack the experience to think of such a thing. But you might be carrying my heir. Not a small consideration."

"You knew it though. You didn't use protection."

"There is no need. I assumed that your desire for me was your agreement."

"And here we are again, back to your ego. Wanting your body has nothing to do with wanting to spend the rest of my life with you."

"But it will be a royal marriage, Mouse. That means we might manage to see very little of each other. If you so desire."

"Why do you want to marry me?" she asked. "You could have asked any woman. Any random woman on the street might have said yes."

"Because I need you," he said, the words coming out so rough they surprised even him. "I do not know how to be a man without you. I do not know what I would do if you were not in my life, and that trip we took just before Violet cried off our engagement only underlined that. You are what this country needs. They need you more than they need me. *I* need you." It was true, for he did not possess a soul, not a real one. But she did.

"Matteo, you don't need me. Not like that."

Her rejection of the honesty he had not wanted to issue enraged him. It was poison to admit his need and now she was telling him it was not real.

"Livia, look at us. Look at *this*. Are you going to sit there and defend my humanity even now? I'm a monster, but a monster who craves you nonetheless, and I will not leave you for another man to devour. That simple. That base."

"You're a stubborn ass, but that doesn't make you a monster."

"Even now you think so?"

"Yes, even now. Matteo," she said, feeling defeated now. "Don't I deserve a chance at a life?"

"I am offering you a life beyond any you could have had on your own. And no, not because I will be your husband. Because you will be Queen. Think of all that you can accomplish."

"I have accomplished a lot," she said, sounding weary. "I had thought that for a while I could just live."

The weary words settled between them.

"Some people are not meant for that," he said. "Some people are meant for greatness. It was always going to be us, Liv," he said, her name hoarse in his throat. "It was always going to be this, don't you agree?"

His chest felt painful with the truth of it. With the years laid out honest and clean behind him so he could see, truly, how inevitable it was.

"You were meant to be Queen, from the moment you were born. And it was a hard road getting here, but I believe you were born to it the same that I was. That from the very beginning, you were chosen, by fate, by the universe, to be the Queen, and it is why I saw you that day when I was driving along the streets. And it is why you came with me. Why you seemed fated to be in the palace, why everything you touched turned to gold. Perhaps it is why Violet and Javier think they are in love. Perhaps it is not they who are meant to be, so much as us. Because you are meant for great things. Greater than just living."

A tear spilled down her cheek. "What a very lofty thing to claim for someone else's life."

"Is it so very lofty?" he asked. "Compared to everything you do all the time? You are... You are an exceptional creature, Livia, why would you ever seek to be ordinary?"

"I've never been ordinary," she said. "I suppose maybe when you have never had the experience, it's what you dream of."

There was a need in her eyes that made him feel less than a king. Less than a man. He hated it. Hated that he had no idea what to do for her.

"I don't know that I have ever dreamed."

She looked up at him. "Never?"

He laughed. "How could I?"

"I don't know."

"Tell me, Livia," he demanded. "Tell me your dreams."

If it was a white horse, a white peacock, a closet of garments, he could make it so. He wanted to know that he could fulfill her dreams.

He wanted to know he could answer that need but he feared it would not be so simple.

"My nightmares are always being left at the carnival. My mother took me there when I was ten years old. A treat. The sort of thing we never did. For she had always taught me to be wary and distrustful of the outside world. We spent very little time in it. But I had seen a carnival one day, and I had told her I really wished to go. I was always asking for things. I think… in hindsight, I always wanted too much. And she felt defeated by such things, for we had nothing. Nothing. She struggled to feed me. Struggled to keep me happy. I did not go to school. What I learned, I learned on my own. Picking up books and asking those around me if they knew the sounds the letters made. And I wanted… I wanted more than the life that we had. I wanted too much. She used to tell me that. 'You want too much, Livia. The world does not exist to serve you.'" Livia blinked hard. "And one day, she took me to the carnival. I hadn't even asked. Not that day, and I was stunned. She bought me cotton candy, and it was the first time I had ever tried it. It was wonderful, and I was distracted, taken in by all the lights and colors and the sweetness of the treat. And then she was gone. I looked for her everywhere. I looked for her for days. I was thrown out of the carnival when they closed at night, and I stayed by the gates. Crying. Things were different then… There were no police particularly concerned with my plight. When your father ruled it was a military state, and the health and wellness of children crying on the street were hardly a real concern. But you know that. I waited. She didn't return. And I finally realized… I realized when I went back to our camp, after days of walking, and they were gone, that she had meant to leave me behind. I don't know what she told the rest of the people. If she told them anything at all. We are meant largely to govern ourselves, and so…"

Rage filled him. Fueled him.

She might not have told him her dreams, but he could work with her nightmares.

His lip curled. *Of course.* A monster could work much more easily with nightmares.

"Don't you think your mother deserves nothing less than for you to become her Queen?" he asked, anger on behalf of Livia burning in his gut.

How do you have the right to be angry for her? You kidnapped her.

Yes, he had. But only because it was for her own good. And surely it wouldn't take long for her to understand that. For her to see it.

"You can be the Queen your people deserve. And your mother will know. Don't you think she will recognize you? And if you tell your story, of how you were a girl abandoned, who became Queen, she will hear. She will know that's her daughter. The one she said wanted too much. Only to have it all. Only to have the whole world at her feet. The entire country. What do you think of that?"

"I think…" The words were choked in her throat. "I do not know that I can live my life for those kinds of motivations."

"Don't you think we could be happy in some regard? Don't you think…"

"I don't know."

"What were you going to do with your life if you did not marry me? You were going to stay my assistant until I proposed?"

She looked up at him, exhaustion on her face.

"I'm tired," she said. "I do not wish to be badgered. Leave me alone." And then she curled up on the seat as if he had been dismissed, and buried her face in the butter-soft leather. Whether or not she was actually asleep he couldn't tell, but she was certainly doing a great impression of a person who might be.

An hour later, they landed on the grounds of the palace in Monte Blanco. He had gotten dressed on the plane, and had arranged for all of Livia's things to be sent back to the palace. He had also dealt with her lease on the apartment. It was now in his name.

She would be furious. He hadn't wanted her to lose the place, if she wanted it as a little bolt-hole, or a vacation spot for them… He found it slightly underwhelming, but he was not going to take from her what she wanted.

When the plane landed, he woke her.

She gave him a mean-eyed stare, anger the first emotion on her face, even coming out of dreams.

"We are here."

She sat. Unmoving.

"If you don't think I will carry you into the palace, you are mistaken."

"I think you should have to do it. I think that everyone should know."

"Oh, Mouse, that you think I might balk at that shows that you do not know me half as well as you think. And here you made such bold claims about understanding me. No. You understood my civilized façade. Because it is the one you helped create. But you do not understand me. I have been cut open in the darkness. I have been asked to endure unimaginable amounts of pain. Do you know what sort of humiliation comes with that? It is endless. To be my father's own personal canvas of destruction. But I never gave in to his desire to see me weep. I never gave him what he wanted. The screams that he demanded. I withstood all the interrogation meant to simulate foreign invaders. Like I said, I just think he was a sociopath. A psychopath perhaps. Because he seemed to enjoy it. But I withstood all these things, and you think you know what created me? You think you know what will make me flinch? You think that you can shame me by forcing me to carry you into the palace?" He laughed. And then he picked her up from her seat and held her in his arms like a child, as the door to the plane lowered and their feet touched Monte Blancan soil.

Then, the two of them entered the palace, though she not on her own feet. Every member of staff looked away discreetly. He carried her back to her own bedchamber. "I will be back to speak to you. You have time to change and get yourself together. There will be instructions that you are not to leave, though, so I suggest that you not try. You will not be leaving the country. You will not be leaving the palace."

Then he turned and left her, heading straight toward his brother's offices. He found Javier sitting at his desk, with Violet perched on a love seat, taking a picture of herself.

"I have returned," he said.

"So you have," Javier responded.

Violet looked up at him. "Did you leave?"

"I brought Livia back."

"Did you?" Javier asked.

"Yes. We are to be married."

"She said yes?" Violet asked.

"Not exactly."

"What do you mean not exactly?" Javier asked.

"Oh, I've kidnapped her. She is shut in her rooms, and the entire staff will be given strict instructions not to allow her to leave. Also, she is on a no-fly list for the country."

"Madre de Dios," Javier said. "You know you can't do that."

"But I have." He shrugged. "So it seems that I can."

"That is not the way to start a marriage," Violet said.

"Well," Javier said. "Actually, that is how we began ours. With kidnap."

"Kidnap should not be quite so common," Violet said grumpily.

"It is how we solve our problems."

"Perhaps you should try *talking* about your feelings," Violet said.

Matteo and Javier exchanged a glance, and both of them chuckled.

"That is silly," Matteo said.

"That is rather silly," Javier agreed.

"We talk about our feelings all the time," Violet said.

"I might talk about them with you," Javier said. "But I will go to great lengths to not discuss them with my brother more than is humanly possible."

"I do not have feelings."

"Clearly you have some, or you would not have gone to such an extent to bring Livia back."

"She is the best choice to be Queen of the country. Actually, it's perfect. Because she is better at diplomacy than you will ever be, no offense," he said, directing that at Violet.

"None taken."

"And we still retain the benefit of your presence here in the country. Truly, I could not have planned it better. And you know that pains me to say it. That fate might have better plans than I do. I like to fancy myself as being supreme director of all things. But sometimes, you simply must acknowledge that a twist of fate has produced something even better."

"Wow," Violet said.

"I expect your support in all of this," he said, addressing both of them.

"I will not support your kidnap of your assistant."

"Neither will I," Javier said.

"You have to," he said, directing that at Javier. "Because you kidnapped Violet. And look how you ended up."

"We are in love. That's different."

"Livia was going to stay here at the palace anyway. She is simply out of sorts over the marriage aspect. God knows why."

"It's as if you're impossible and frustrating," Violet said sweetly.

"Is my brother not?"

"Well…"

"That's what I thought. Anyway. She is here. And the marriage will proceed. Whether she says yes or not."

"And when it comes to actually exchanging vows? What do you intend to do then?"

"I am a king. The marriage can be binding however I choose it to be. I could write up a document that I signed myself stating that I married her, and it would be done."

He supposed he ought to feel…something. About the fact that he was being quite such an autocrat. But he would not be bad to her. In fact, he would treat her as if she were… As if she were Queen. But she would be. So there was no reason for guilt. None whatsoever.

And for him, control was essential.

"I'm sorry," Javier said. "But I will not allow it. And I am second in command in this country, and the head of your military, and I will have to see that Livia has agreed to the marriage before I will allow it to proceed."

"Or you will start a war with me?"

"Yes. To prevent you from engaging with an even bigger one inside of yourself. You do not wish to be this leader."

He growled. "Do not tell me what I wish." He turned and stalked out of the room, going straight back to Livia.

She gasped when he opened the chamber door, and held the T-shirt to her breast. She was wearing a pair of sweatpants, and a bra.

"A bit late for belated shows of modesty, don't you agree?"

"What are you doing here?"

"I'm here to speak to you of marriage."

She let out a growl, and jerked the top over her head.

"Be reasonable."

"Why should I marry you?"

And somehow, even with all the reasons, all the logic that existed inside of him, there was only one answer that came to him. Only one that resonated in his soul.

"Because I want you."

And then Livia let out a cry, closed the space between them and flung herself into his arms.

CHAPTER TEN

THIS WAS FOLLY. It was disastrous. And she couldn't stop herself. Because what he had said, so ragged and raw, was the first thing that had actually resonated within her.

Oh, yes, it had been very tempting when he asked her about her mother. When he had asked if she would enjoy it if the woman knew that Livia was now her Queen. She was only human. And it was an enticement to a girl who had spent a great many nights dreaming about all the ways she might show her mother she had never needed her.

And he'd known that. Had known of a way to cut down deep into her soul.

He was good at that. Unfortunately.

But this.

Raw and honest, this was what she could not deny.

She had thought that she could make love with him once and walk away?

She had been a fool.

And not because she had imagined he would pick her up and fling her over his shoulder and kidnap her, but because she was bound to him. Whether he had done it or not.

She hadn't made a very good sport of trying to escape him. And in truth... He could've taken her hand and led her down to that car, led her onto the plane, and she probably would've gone.

Because she was only human.

She was only a woman. A woman who had loved one man for a very long time. Who'd had to flee a country in order to keep herself from capitulating to him too easily.

But he had come after her. She had run away, and he had been right there behind her. And she had given in. Folded herself into him with no great resistance at all.

And she had told herself all kinds of lies.

But now, with him holding her like this, she could see them for what they were.

It was all such a farce.

As if she could ever refuse him. She loved him too much. And this was far too close to a perfect dream than anything else Livia had ever had.

She had never been able to find her people again. She had never seen her mother. She had never known her father. She had spent nine years in fear, yearning, and then...

He was offering her a chance to be Queen. He

was offering her his hand, even though he was not offering her his heart. So she kissed him. Like she might be drowning, and he was there to save her. Kissed him as if her life depended on it, and in the moment, it felt like it did.

Kissed him until his hands created all manner of pleasure and fire that consumed the uncertainty inside of her.

She had known this man for years, loved him. But there were still dark places in him she could sense but could not see.

And she wanted to see them. Wanted to see him. For better or worse.

"Say yes," he growled.

"Yes," she said, tears pouring down her cheeks.

She had lost. She had lost the battle inside of herself but she had won him, so wasn't that fine? Wasn't it okay?

What she was tired of was fighting. Pure and simple. Of wanting and not having. Of being in a constant state of deprivation.

So yes, the idea of being Queen, of being his wife who would never have his heart, had notes of exhaustion buried inside of it, but so did this. A life spent without Matteo. The nine years that she had carried wanting him, needing him, and never having him… It was not less exhausting. And if she could not have him now, then it would all have been for nothing. So she had lost at some things. And perhaps it was not so bad to surrender.

She thought of him reaching out his hand when she had been a girl. Seventeen years old and alone on the streets. Refusing him then would have been foolish. Was refusing him now any better? Sometimes you had to take the offered hand, even not knowing where it might lead. Because otherwise you would simply stay in the same spot, and that wasn't always good either.

Maybe that was all fanciful justification, but it amounted to the same thing. She could not turn away from Matteo. And more to the point, she didn't want to.

So, she kissed him. Kissed him until she couldn't breathe. Luxuriated in the feel of his mouth against hers, his gorgeous, hard body the sheltering place she had never had while living on the street.

He gave her so much. So much more than she could have ever hoped to have. Why did she insist on asking for everything?

Everything was…

She was a girl who had come up from a place of wanting only to survive.

She did not need more than being Queen.

She was selfish. And she was fanciful.

Because you look at him and he makes you believe that you could have everything.

No. This was everything. It was all she needed.

He stripped her comfortable clothes away from her body, and she made quick work of his. She'd not had the time to examine the full glory of his male form last night. Last night had been frantic, and it had felt like the end of something.

This, this was just the beginning. This really was a promise she was making, not only to him but to herself.

That she would be thankful for what she had been given, that she would do her best with what fate had set out before her. Because it really was sort of a miraculous thing, and there was no purpose in keeping herself from it.

He laid her down on the glorious, velvet bedspread that she loved so much—she had left it behind when she had gone to Paris. She had been willing to leave so many things behind—for what was a preferred bedspread when she was leaving behind the only man she had ever cared for?—and covered her body with his.

She moved her hands over the muscles on his back, the raised ridges of scars there. And when he raised up slightly, she ran her hands over the scars on his front too. Then she leaned in, kissing them. Tracing the line that she knew his father's knife had followed across his skin. As if she might heal it with her touch.

With the love that burned in her breast, whether she wanted it to be there or not.

Perhaps it would be easier to simply not love him. She knew that Javier and Matteo loved each other as brothers. She knew that they cared, but they did not show that caring in an effusive way. She was the only one that could ever love Matteo like this. And she did not want to hold it back, not now.

All of a sudden, she wanted to pour it out over him. Make him feel it. For hadn't he brought her into the palace and into a sense of safety that she had never known possible? She had spent all these years trying to earn her place, but perhaps she simply needed to be thankful for it. And she was. She was so immensely grateful for all that he had given to her, and it made her want to give no less than she had received.

She wished she could heal him. She really did. Wished that her kisses would penetrate not only his scars, but the hardness of his heart.

But she would take the feel of his body trembling beneath her touch, she would take the apparent arousal that he felt as she moved her hands over his skin, her lips.

She kissed a path down his chest, down his stomach, down to that most masculine part of him. He was glorious. Beautiful.

She had not been prepared to think a man's body was half so beautiful as his was, but it was. A glorious work of art. Carved from the white mountains of their country. Carved from the hardship that he had endured. Weakness. That was the thing he feared most. Not pain. Not death or defeat. Weakness.

That his father might have found a way to make him weak. And what hurt her the most was that she knew that he had.

Whether Matteo could ever see it that way or not...

He had taken away Matteo's ability to feel. Because he had made his son fear that that might be the biggest weakness of all. No. Matteo would never be weak in that way. He was a good man. It was only that he feared himself so deeply.

But when you had been shaped and formed by a monster, how could you do anything else?

She knew that. She knew him.

She worried enough about her own value, her own worth, because of what her mother had done.

And it hurt.

You did not simply unlearn those things, you did not simply unfeel them.

It was not half so simple.

But this was, at least. This desire that she felt for him. And this was an easy way to show him. Because he could understand this. He could feel this.

She caressed him, running her palm over his hardness. Luxuriating in the feel of him beneath her hand.

Oh, but he was a glorious man. Truly wonderful and miraculous in ways that she could not express fully. Not without touch.

So she squeezed him, tested his length. He was large. If she had examined him too closely prior to their first joining she might have been terrified.

But then of course, Matteo de la Cruz could never be anything but exceptional. And he was.

Then she leaned in, his musky, masculine scent tormenting her, enticing her. To greater exploration. She pressed her lips to his shaft, then tasted him tentatively, before taking him fully into her mouth.

He jerked beneath her, and she took control of this moment. Of their pleasure.

All the while, he reached between her thighs and began to test her wetness. Her desire for him. He pushed two fingers inside of her as she continued to taste him, and she let out a low moan of pleasure, which made him growl out his own.

Then he grabbed hold of her, his large hands spanning her waist and easily lifting her up, bringing her down to straddle his body.

"Go right ahead, Mouse. Show me what you can do."

Her heart pounding hard, she shifted, and felt the blunt head of his erection against the entrance to her body. And with shaking thighs, she lowered herself onto him slowly, achingly so. And he filled her, inch by delicious inch. She gasped as he did, her head thrown back on a sigh of pleasure.

"Show me," he growled. "Show me what you want, Livia."

She shifted her hips tentatively, finding a slow and steady rhythm until pleasure began to build inside of her to an unbearable degree. Her core ached with need, her body so slick, the friction it created driving her near to the brink. And then, he seemed to lose his control entirely. He thrust up into her, arching up off the bed, the ferocity of his movements pushing her over. Her internal muscles pulsed around him, and she couldn't hold back the scream of her release, didn't want to. For she wanted him to know. Wanted him to know just how deeply she was affected by this. By the intensity of their joining.

His own feral growl of release was not far behind, his blunt fingers digging hard into her hips, and she was certain there would be bruises there.

Good. She wanted to be marked by it. Wanted to be changed by it. She wanted to wear it.

For she had wanted this, wanted him for an untold number of years.

And when it was done, she lay, spent and breathing hard against his chest.

And she felt… Happy.

For all that this was imperfect, for all that they were imperfect, there was a deep sort of satisfaction to this that she had never known before.

"Would you like anything?" he asked, his voice rough.

A smile curved her lips. "Coffee."

And that was how she found herself naked, sitting

in her bed drinking coffee with Matteo. It was a direct echo of that night she had found him dreaming.

And it was a relief, because it was something other than the fighting and all of his autocratic behavior from the previous few days. This was where he was human. She liked him something more than human too. It was part of his charm after all. Perhaps charm was overstating it. But it was part of him. A man who was bigger than life. A man who was nearly a god. A rock. A mountain.

But also a man.

"When you were a child," he said, "what did you dream? Before there were nightmares. Before… Before everything. What was all that *too much* that you wanted?"

"I dreamed of education. I dreamed of a world where we didn't have to be afraid of the King. Where we did not have to hide from soldiers."

"I'm sorry."

"It isn't your fault. My people are freer now than they've ever been, and that is because of you."

"And you will continue it," he said. "I'm confident in that."

"I hope so. I hope I will be a good queen."

"You will marry me, then."

"It enrages me to say, since I know you were nothing but confident in it this whole time."

"I was not," he said softly. "I questioned it. The thing about you, Livia, is that I have never been able to anticipate what you would do. You are a constant source of surprise, Mouse. And very few people are that to me. If anyone. For I realized when I was very young that no matter what façade a person presented to the world, they could be anything beneath it. My father never looked like a good king, but I'm not convinced he looked entirely like the sociopath he was behind the scenes. I don't think anyone would have ever guessed that he would play havoc with the body of his heir, for example."

She shook her head. "No. I don't suppose. You would think that he would have valued you. That he would've protected you above all else."

"Perhaps that was what he told himself. That he was building me into a resilient super soldier of some kind. Though I doubt it."

"And what of your dreams?"

"I did not have any. I was born into darkness, and I felt as if I would continue to live in it no matter what. That there would be no escaping it. After all, my father was my blood. And he told me, repeatedly, that I would be the same manner of king that he is. He made it clear that his goal was to transform me into another part of him. He said his father before him was the same, and his father before him. So why would I have any chance of being different? I knew that I had to make a choice. And it wasn't a dream. It was simply… Determination. I saw the suffering of my people and I regretted it bitterly. So

I bided my time. I gave no indication that I might be different. And then… And then when it was my time, I set about to change things. But you are right, I didn't know how to interact with people. I mostly still don't. For I had to learn to hide everything, to keep it hidden, to keep it pushed down, otherwise… What my father could see, he would exploit. What he could touch, he would damage. What he could fight against, he would. And I cannot allow that to be so."

"How do you know? That there is something else out there in the world when you are born into a specific environment that does not allow you to see a reality that's different from yours?"

"I might ask you the same, Livia. You certainly didn't know that there was a world out there where you could have education. You must not have known your own potential. Here you are, on the verge of being Queen. Surely you could not have known that, and yet dared to want better. And you fought to survive on the streets, not even knowing if you would ever find a different sort of reality than the one that you had been thrust into. How exhausting it must be, to fight so hard to simply survive."

"Yes. I didn't just dream of that. I dreamed of candy and cake and living. Of gowns, of parties. A birthday party. I had my very first birthday party that I can ever remember here at the palace. It was magic. I wanted so many pretty things, and I do worry…"

"What is it?"

"That part of me wishes to be Queen because I will have beautiful dresses and I will be pampered and cared for and I will have all of the sex that I could ever want, and I will be so comfortable. And isn't that quite selfish?"

"There is nothing wrong with wanting all of those things. Particularly not when you have been deprived as you've been."

"Well. Now you know. I am quite only human."

"You are quite the most amazing human."

"Thank you. Matteo… What about children?"

"I must have them," he said.

"Yes. But you have told me, many times over the years, that your heart is stone. That you cannot feel emotion because of what happened to you. I understand that. I… I do." She might not accept it, but she did understand it. She might not think it was right, but she could understand it. "But what about *our* children?"

She wanted to cry. Admitting, accepting that this would mean having children with Matteo. Having children at all, when that was a dream that she had never even thought to entertain.… It was wonderful. Wonderful and emotional and terrifying all at once.

"I will be good to them. And I will show them the path that they should walk on. And you… Livia, you are the only person who has ever given me the sort of care that you did. You will be the best mother. My mother vanished from my life when I was too young to remember her clearly. And I always feared asking what had become of her. Now I will never know. But you… You will be there for our children. A gift that neither of us had. That is enough for me."

Her heart felt like it might burst. And she knew that she should be suspicious of this, knew that she should be on her guard, knew that she should protect herself, but she didn't have the energy to do it. In this moment, she simply wanted to sink into it. Simply wanted to revel in it and be.

"I will do my very best," she said. "To treat them as neither of us were."

"We will be married as soon as possible," he said, resolute.

"Yes," she agreed.

"I will go back to my room now," he said.

"No," she said. "Stay with me."

He looked at her, his dark eyes unfathomable. Then she saw in it an emotion, so deep and raw that it was nearly terrifying to look at directly.

"Being married does not mean you have to share a room with me. That is not how royal marriages typically work."

"No. But I should like for us to share a room. What do you think of that?"

"Then we shall," he said.

He took the coffee cup in her hand and set it along with his own on the nightstand. "Come to me, my Queen."

And she thought, as she gave herself over to him, that being Queen Mouse might not be so bad after all.

He awoke in the dark. Gasping, sweating. The pain was unbearable. But then, cool hands were on his skin, a soft mouth pressed to his scars.

He had never fallen asleep with a woman before. Never. For this reason. But she was there. And she comforted him. And he knew immediately who it was. Livia. His Mouse.

His Queen.

Comforting him in the way that only she could.

It had been so from the beginning.

It was a weakness, perhaps, to need this the way that he did.

But he wasn't sure he cared.

For he was too caught up in it, in her touch, and the soothing words that she spoke. He pulled her to him, and kissed her. Kissed her with all the rising, angry emotion in his chest.

No. It was only in his dreams that he ever felt this. During the day, he walked around with the rock where his heart should be. During the day, he remembered who he was, what he must be.

It was only now, only now at night that things became muddled and fuzzy. But she was so soft, his Livia.

Livia.

For it had always been her. *He would've married another woman.*

Right then, in the darkness of their room, in this shared bed, with his nightmares fresh on his heels and his body burning from the pain woven out of his dreams, he felt destroyed by that thought.

That he might've made another woman his Queen. *Livia* was his Queen.

On this line between sleep and wakefulness it seemed so clear. She kissed him, matching his desperation. And when he turned her over and sank into her welcoming body, everything seemed bright. Everything seemed to make sense. Everything seemed to be as it had never been before. His chest felt like it might burst, and he found that he could not breathe.

He felt as if she might have answers. And she might have had those same answers on that night so many years ago, when she had first come to him.

Livia.

His.

His woman.

CHAPTER ELEVEN

MATTEO MOVED ALL of her things into his chamber shortly after that.

And the plans for the wedding were proceeding at pace. Livia couldn't deny that she felt a certain amount of disquiet over the whole thing. Mostly because... Well, she was used to fading into the background. And now... She wouldn't be.

Matteo had made an announcement to his people, that Livia was going to be Queen. And it was all done now. There was no turning back. She'd said yes to him. She would've been disappointed in herself if she were not quite so satisfied in other ways.

She was sitting in the dining room, having an afternoon espresso, when Violet walked in. Violet, who would be her sister-in-law. Violet, whom she had resented so much not that long ago.

It was strange. How much things had changed so quickly. She had liked Violet almost immediately, that had been difficult, when she'd been mired in her jealousy.

Jealousy she'd gotten over immediately when she'd seen how Violet loved Javier. It had been easy for them to find a friendship after that.

"Hi," Violet said.

"Hello," Livia responded.

"How is everything going with the wedding plans?"

A staff member came in, and Violet requested her own espresso, and some cake.

"I might have some cake," Livia said.

"Of course," the woman responded.

"Is it strange?" Violet asked. "To go from... working here to..."

Livia blinked. "Well, yes. Though, honestly it's all happened so slowly. I've been with Matteo for nine years. I mean, not *been* with... I... I've been here at the palace. And things have evolved."

"Yes," Violet said. "They truly have. I haven't been here very long. And things with Javier moved quite quickly. But... That wasn't the case for you."

Livia looked away. "I loved him... For a very long time."

"You must be happy, then. That it has worked out this way."

"I'm not sure anything is worked out yet."

"Why not? You're marrying him."

"Yes. I'm marrying him." Javier and Violet were in love. In love in a way Matteo said they could not be. But somehow Javier loved. She was desperate to know more about that. "You know… Javier must've had a very difficult time with his feelings."

"Yes. He did. Did Matteo not tell you how things were for Javier?"

"Some small things. I know about Matteo's experiences, but not Javier's. He guards that relationship. Between himself and his brother. I think it is the only lifelong relationship he's ever had that meant anything to him. No, I don't think that, I know it. He cares for Javier very much, but showing feelings is hard for him."

"He has always seemed…" Violet looked thoughtful. "Granted I don't know him that well, but he has always seemed easier than Javier. I was quite annoyed of myself that it was Javier who captured my attention. Considering he was my jail keeper, and a grump."

"Matteo hides it. But he's very…" She thought of his scars. She thought of his nightmares. All of those things she would keep to herself. For it was his story. And it was not hers to share. She would never uncover him in such a way.

They had trust between them that he didn't share with anyone else, and she would never do anything to violate that.

"You know about their father. Their mother was gone before either of them could have ever known her. And their father was not a good man. Javier trusted him, Matteo never did. But Matteo saw the worst of him. And he is… It's like emotion doesn't touch him. As if everything glances off. It's why he seems an easier man. He does not easily feel anything half so intense as anger."

But things between them were intense enough, and there was no denying that. They felt plenty for each other. At least, in bed.

"He believes it is how a king must be."

"I see. And so… His view of love…"

"Dim," she said. "Actually, I don't think he believes he can feel it."

"And you?"

"I know I can," Livia said.

"Are you happy, though, with the prospect of marrying him?"

"I am… I would not be happy had he married anyone else, that much is certain. But I… I'm afraid."

"You don't have to marry him," Violet said softly. "I know he wants you to, and I understand that you love him, and that you want him, but you don't have to simply take what's on offer."

"But what other choice do I have? I would be miserable without him." She sighed heavily. "I already tried to leave. I didn't stay gone."

"Sure, but you deserve to be loved," Violet said. "Not just to give it, but to get it back."

"But he deserves to be loved," Livia said. "And

I think I'm the only one that can love him the way that I do."

"He should become the only man who can love you as he does. And as much as I care for him, as he is my brother-in-law, and I do know that he and my husband had a terrible time in their youth… I really do think that he might have to work for something, for feelings, to ever be able to heal. It would not be good for him to simply be given everything he asks for, and not be required to change at all."

"He's changed," Livia said, feeling defensive.

"If you say so. I don't want you to leave, Livia, to be very clear. I like having you here, and I think now we have become friends. But should you not have everything?"

"Some people just can't have everything."

She repeated what she had told herself only last night.

"No," Violet said. "That isn't true. Somebody who loves as ferociously as you absolutely deserves to have everything. It doesn't matter what happened in your past. It doesn't matter what other people have made you feel about yourself. How small they've made you feel. How insecure it's made you feel. None of it is true. It doesn't get to decide what you become. The only person that can decide to accept less is you."

"What if it isn't less?" she whispered. "I mean…

I was nothing. I was on the streets. He's going to make me a queen. And I... I love him."

"The real concern is if you are allowing him to accept less. What if he could feel more? Not for another woman, don't mistake me. But if you asked for more, what if he had to dig inside himself and heal?"

She didn't know what to say to that. "But I want to marry him," she said, after their cake had been left sitting in front of them.

"Then you should."

"Well, you just made it sound like you thought I shouldn't."

"No. It's only that I want you to be happy. That I want both of you to be happy. That's all. I'm really not telling you what to do. Maybe it's hormones. I should probably be ignored. Anyway," Violet said, a slight smile curving her lips. "There is a very interesting Royal wedding night tradition in Monte Blanco."

"Is there?"

"Yes. It involves jeweled handcuffs." Violet made eye contact with her as she took a sip of her espresso. "If nothing else, it's worth getting to that point just for the experience."

"Only on the wedding night?" Livia asked.

"No," she said. "Javier finds excuses to use them whenever he is of a mood. Which is often."

Was it so wrong to want this? Violet had made her question it, and yet Violet's presence was part of what made Livia want this. She could have a sister-in-law. A friend. Right here in the palace. She could have… Royal wedding nights complete with hand-cuffs. She could have so much here.

But not love.

Maybe love was overrated. Maybe it didn't matter.

It was all fine for Violet and her American sensibilities to feel like it was something that Livia should be fighting for. But maybe she could just… Maybe she could just have this. And it would be enough.

It was time for the pre-wedding festivities to begin. All of it was a bit much for Matteo's taste, but he also did not see why he would change the protocol. He did not want to offend Livia in any way, and he had the feeling that were he to back off on the festivities, she would take it as a sign that somehow she was less important to him than another queen might have been, and not simply that he did not care for seven days' worth of pageantry.

Which was the truth of it.

He had not seen her all day. She was being treated, royally, in order to come out gleaming and wrapped in velvet, and worthy of her position as Queen, though in his opinion, she was already far beyond worthy. It wasn't until it was nearly time to go into the ballroom that he saw her for the first time. Uncharacteristically, her hair was down, falling in soft waves just past her shoulders. Her makeup was light, illuminating her face, rather than covering it. As much as he had liked the red lipstick she'd worn the other night, he liked this version of her. This one that was familiar but gleaming and special all at the same time.

She was wearing green. A strapless, velvet gown with a neckline that plunged down between her glorious breasts, and he wanted to cover her, because he did not want anyone else to see what was his.

"Hi," she said, looking almost shy. She looked down, her pale lashes fanning across her cheekbones.

"I would rather take you to our bedroom, than into the ballroom," he said.

"Oh," she answered.

"I heard… I did hear… That is to say… Violet said something about handcuffs?"

The idea warmed his blood. He had thought little about the tradition in Monte Blanco of binding the bride's wrists and ankles on the wedding night, but he was thinking of it now. And found it quite overly appealing. Oh, yes, he would enjoy exploring those sensual delights with Livia. The games that could be made out of restraints would be lush, and the very thought sent a kick of desire through him.

"I used to scrub these floors," she said, as they stood before the ballroom doors.

"And you never will again," he said.

No. He wished to elevate her and keep her there.

This beautiful, incomparable woman who was his in every way.

His.

The doors opened for them, and they entered the room. It was already filled with peacocks, guests dressed in finery from head to toe. Laughing and drinking and dancing. His brother was there, and he was actually smiling, with Violet on his arm, looking stunning in the color that was her namesake. But he could not imagine her on his arm. And he could only be grateful, yet again, that she and Javier had found each other, so that he could stand here with Livia.

As they walked into the room, a hush fell over it, and he found that even the members of staff in attendance were staring at them. At her.

But of course, it must be notable, that she was among them, not so long ago, and now she was to be their Queen.

He wondered how that would be for her. But then, if there was even a whisper of disrespect among the staff, he would have them removed at once.

Livia had suffered enough in her life, and there was no need for her to suffer anymore. He would see to that. He would never allow anyone to make her feel like she was less, not ever again.

They moved deeper into the room, and it took a while, but soon Livia began to loosen, began to warm, and the way that she had been on their previous trip started to come into the fore. He could see that she would do well at this. He was confident in it. And he was prouder of her than he had ever been of anyone or anything in all of his life.

She was an amazing creature. And she was his.

He was waylaid by heads of state, and Livia kept on walking, greeting others in attendance. He kept watch on her out of the corner of his eye, but trusted she would do well.

And she did. She was not shy, nor was she unaccustomed to many of the guests.

Suddenly, she jolted, as one of the men in attendance bumped into her and spilled a drink over the bodice of her gown.

"Oh," she said. "I'm sorry… I…"

"Perhaps you should clean it yourself," the man said. "As you are only a maid, after all."

Matteo found himself moving toward her without thought.

He was across the space immediately, his blood pounding like a hammer. "Clean this up," he said to the man. "Who are you?"

"A reporter, Your Majesty."

"For?"

"Monte Blanco Press."

"And you are no longer employed there, I will ensure that. Now, see yourself out of the palace."

Everything had stopped in the room. Everyone was listening to him. Was watching.

"Your Majesty…"

"There is no argument. If this is not clean and you are not gone in the next few moments I will see you thrown in the dungeon. Have no doubts, there is still a dungeon here. Do you think I fear to use it? I may not be the same King as my father, but I will not tolerate disrespect. You will respect my Queen. As she *is* to be your Queen. And it does not matter where she came from, she is above you. She always has been. You are nothing. And I could destroy you with a mere word."

The man had gone pale, and Matteo didn't care. He wanted the man to be fearful. For his life. For he would pay for this insult to Livia.

"Matteo," she said, putting her hand on his arm. "Stop. Please."

"He dared insult you," Matteo said. "At your own party. And I will have it known this will not stand."

"And I appreciate it," Livia said. "But these are not medieval times, and he can say whatever he wishes. Does he not have the freedom to do so?"

"No," Matteo growled.

"He must," she said. "Or we are no better than we were. He must have the freedom to insult me, as I have the freedom to respond or not respond as I see fit. And I choose not to respond. For I have been through much worse than a few casual insults hurled at me by a man unhappy with his life. And I will endure more scathing commentary, I'm certain. It's true," she said, her voice rising above all other sounds in the ballroom. "I was a maid here. I was a street urchin and one of the forest people before that. I am nothing. And I am now to be Queen. And I will not forget where I came from. I am an advocate for those who do not have a voice, for those who do not have power. This I promise. I will never forget."

She turned to Matteo. "I beg of you. Do not take his job from him."

"He was not able to perform it," Matteo said. "He spilled a drink, on you, and insulted you."

"Yes," Livia said. "And one thing neither you nor I ever got in life was grace. You have a chance to extend it now. Please, Matteo, do it for me."

"No. Get out. It is a wonderful thing that my wife will not forget where she came from. It is why I'm marrying her. But I will not forget from what *I* came from. I'm not a man to be trifled with. You can say whatever you wish, but it will be met with consequences if it is in my hearing. Out."

He could not allow this. Livia deserved better. And there were things he could not give to her, but he could demand her respect.

And the man left. Nearly running out the ballroom door. "Resume festivities," Matteo said.

And as if he had flipped a switch, everyone went back to talking.

Livia looked at him with round, wounded eyes. "Why did you do that?"

"I will have respect. As will you. You are my chosen bride and..."

"And what? And *what*, Matteo? You will exercise your position as king to be a tyrant?"

His chest pitched, heaved.

"I told you already. I do not know another place to be. I was formed by a tyrant. A master manipulator, an evil man. Did you think that I would truly be above any of those things? I am not, nor will I be. I am simply a man. And men can be made into monsters."

Already, these things that he felt for Livia were far too intense.

"We will speak after this."

She was frosty to him for the rest of the evening, and it put him in a foul mood. And when they arrived back at their bedchamber, she rounded on him.

"If I did not wish for him to have such consequences, why did I not get to say?"

"I am the King. Not you. And allowing that kind of disrespect is setting a bad precedent."

"And what consequence comes of it? This is the kind of thing that signals you're an autocrat. That demonstrates to people that you wish to control not only their daily lives but the things they think, the things they say. People will disapprove of me. I did used to be a maid. There's nothing you can do about it."

"I am the King," he said.

"Listen to yourself. This is everything you said you did not want."

He looked at her, realization turning over in his chest. It was true. This was what he had professed he would never be. Not simply an action, but the fact that he had been caught in his own perspective for so many hours now. Deeply convinced of his own rightness. And this was how it began.

This was how it began.

"Matteo," she said. "I know what you came from. And I feel deeply for all that you have endured. But you have it wrong. You don't need to close your heart, you need to open it. You must. At a certain point, you must. If you don't, then it will always be hard like this, and when things happen, when people make mistakes in your presence, they will be nothing but horrendously penalized for it. And you will not be able to see... You won't be able to see. This is the problem. The problem is that you could not understand where his pain was coming from. And that is something I cannot teach you. It's not about putting a smile on your face, it's about learning empathy. He is upset because his own standing in life will not change. He is upset because mine did. It has nothing to do with thinking I am not worthy, so much as he thinks he should have been. It isn't fair. You can accept a certain amount of poverty if you look around you and see others suffering with you, but when someone transcends... It gives you false hope. And this is not a typical trajectory, it is not something other people can dream of. What I was given is not… It is not about my own cleverness. I am made by an act of great mercy shown to me by you. But will all the people get so much mercy shown to them?"

"He is not homeless. He has work. He is not suffering."

"It doesn't matter. It is a feeling of not being able to move positions in life."

"But I think you are wrong," Matteo said. "It is not because I feel nothing, it is because I feel too much."

The words were dragged from him, jagged bits of glass pulled through his chest, his throat. Feelings—good and bad—always existed alongside each other in his heart and he could never separate one from the other.

The trick for him had been to have none and here he was…bleeding with it.

"Matteo…" She put her hand on his arm and looked up at him. "Surely you must know by now how very much I love you."

His whole body went stiff, and his heart turned to stone. Everything in him rejected that simple, softly spoken statement. "No," he said.

"I do. I do love you and…"

"You were warned. You were told. There will be no love between us. Not ever."

Love.

Love was the greatest enemy.

For him, love was toxic.

He wished it didn't exist.

He wished it were so.

"It's too late. There already is. And love is what you need, you hardheaded ass. You need to feel something in that great, mountain of a chest of yours. You cannot be a rock forever."

"I must be a rock, immovable. For it is emotion that caused me to lash out at that man. A sense of anger. Of what I thought to be right, colored by the way I felt. It is not good. I must know what is right, and it must never change, regardless of the circumstances. You are right. I violated all which I had chosen to be in the way that I behaved tonight, and I did it in a room full of people. No. You will not entice me to more feeling, Mouse."

"Then I never did remove the thorn. And I was never your mouse, not really. Because it's still there, festering away, creating a wound that will never, ever heal. You don't want it to heal. You wanted it to sit there, causing you pain, because it makes you feel good to know it's there, because you can protect yourself. And you can say whatever you wish about protecting the kingdom but it isn't the truth. You don't want to feel because then you have to cope with being human. With being vulnerable. And we both know it's the thing you fear most. Making mistakes.

Being seen as weak. Crying out with pain. But…
Perhaps Violet is right. Perhaps it is what you need."

"What does Violet have to do with anything?"

"Never mind. Just tell me… Could you love me?
Do you think there is a chance you could, even a
little bit?"

"It is an impossibility. I cannot love you."

"You cannot? Or you will not?"

"They are the same, for I am a king. And what I
will is simply what is."

The look on her face was devastated, crushed,
but she had known. There was not another person
on earth who knew him half so well as she did.
She should not be surprised. She should not be so
wounded. And he… He should not respond to it.
"We wed tomorrow," he said. "We have the rest of
our lives to disagree."

"I don't want that."

"You're mine," he said. "Mine." And he pulled
her to him and kissed her, fiercely. And she returned
it. Giving back everything he gave to her. Matching
him, with each and every kiss. He stripped her of her
gown and allowed her to strip him of his suit. And
then it was just the two of them, here in his room,
this place where they had compared scars and nightmares. This place where they slept together, tangled
up in each other, just enough that it kept the dreams
away. And this was the only thing he could do now.
The only thing that felt right. For he was a naked

mass of too many feelings, and it was all her fault. This was all her fault. And tonight had demonstrated that what he was afraid of was exactly what would come to pass if he gave in.

Oh, but it was a short bridge, to firing someone and making threats of the dungeon to actually following through with it. To disallowing disloyal talk about the Queen, to demanding total control over a group of people who refused to live under the King's command.

Such a short bridge to what his father had become. And the vision of it now, the clarity there, was a rolling tide of horror.

But her mouth was not. For here things made sense. She made sense.

And so he lost himself. In her. In the softness of her touch. And everything she gave.

And he took.

Greedily. Drank from her mouth, lost himself in her body. And when he thrust deep within her, she let out a gasp. "I love you."

It washed over him like a warm wave. And he could feel it, reaching the parched places of his soul. Could feel how desperate he was.

No.

He could not accept it. He could not.

"I love you," she whispered again as he thrust back inside her. "I love you. I love you. I love you. I love you."

Like the counting off in their dance lesson. Steady and insistent and filled with all the need that he had tried to deny all these years.

He could feel that weakness. Shifting, eroding inside of him.

And suddenly, he felt like a boy. Enduring torture.

But not the kind his father had given out. No. This was like having a cherished dream held out in front of him, only to have it be just out of reach.

Then, he could no longer think. Then, there was nothing but the white-hot pleasure that erupted inside of him, and she cried out as he spilled himself inside of her, as she pulsed around him. And then he worked to harden himself, to go back to what he was.

For a moment, he had her and that would have to be enough. It would have to be, because it was all he could allow.

Livia was his. And she would be as she had been in the ballroom. His conscience. And she would love him.

I was never your mouse...

He shut that out, and he held her close.

Because she was. Whatever she said.

And he would allow no other reality to encroach.

For he decided what it was.

And he was set in this.

And so, it would be.

CHAPTER TWELVE

THE DAY OF the wedding dawned bright and clear, and Livia felt as if there was a storm cloud hanging over her head. She was dressed in a gown of the finest satin, a dream for the girl that she'd been, who had thought that she might have nice things one day.

This was beyond nice.

She was swathed in the fabric, which molded perfectly to her form, and billowed out around her feet. There were small, glass beads sewn into a growing cascade from the bodice down all the way to the floor, where it shimmered as if it had been put together with ice crystals.

She looked beautiful. She felt beautiful. Just as she had felt Matteo's desperation for her last night. But she could not forget what Violet had said to her.

She had nearly told him last night, but she hadn't the strength. Not when he had kissed her.

She had simply wanted to push everything away and be with him. Because it was better. Because it was easier. Easier than dealing with the sad reality of the situation she found herself in.

Everything. Absolutely everything was right at her fingertips except...

Matteo was breaking apart. She could see it. She could see it in the way that he had behaved last night. And she was not... She was not helping him.

She had given so much credit to the fact that she had healed him in some way, but what she'd said last night remained true.

She clearly had not healed him in any meaningful fashion, or...or he would not be so hard, not still.

But there were things that he refused to see. Things that he refused to accept. And that she could not do for him. However, she had a terrible feeling that she might be part of preventing the healing.

She couldn't take that final step for him, but she could certainly keep him comfortable enough that he never took the step for himself.

She looked at herself in the mirror. She was dressed as his bride. Ready to walk down the aisle toward him. Ready to be everything that she had ever dreamed. His Queen. His wife.

Except his love.

She would never be his love.

And she would never know what it was to be loved. She would just be an assistant who had undergone a very fancy promotion. She would not be the wife of his heart. Not really. Not for so long as he denied even having a heart.

She took a deep breath, and picked up her bouquet. And then she saw the time.

The wedding was about to begin.

The massive chapel on the grounds of the palace was filled to capacity. Everyone inside dressed in finery. Women in hats and dresses that brought to mind an array of Easter eggs, the men in fitted suits.

And Matteo stood at the head of the altar and waited. And waited.

For Livia. Always for Livia.

His heart was like a bruised and battered thing, and had been since she'd told him of her love, and still he was here.

Because he could not imagine a future without her.

A future where you cannot give her the one thing she wants...

He was not strong enough to turn away from her.

That was his failing.

That was his shame.

And so he waited.

The music began, and then changed. But Livia did not appear. And even when he was certain that she had missed her cue, she still did not appear.

A hush rippled through the room as he strode back up the aisle and out the doors. "Livia," he shouted. "Livia."

Then he walked to the room where she had been readying herself, only to find it…empty.

Her bouquet was sitting there on the vanity. But there was no note.

But of course, Livia wouldn't leave a note. She would simply do what she had always done.

And it was as if all the blood within him ran free of his body.

He wrenched his tie free and ran from the chapel, making his way toward the palace. Because she couldn't have gone. He would have been notified by the rest of the staff. There was no way she could've simply slipped away.

And when he entered the palace, he met her at the exit. She was wearing black. Her gold spectacles were back on her face. Her hair laughably formal for the attire she was currently garbed in.

"I'm sorry," she said. "But it is for the best."

"Why?"

"Because you don't love me."

"I cannot love anyone. You know that."

"No. It's a lie, and I know it is. And if you cannot love me, then it will be someone else, but I will not do us this disservice. I will not do *you* this disservice." She put her hands on his face. "I love you," she said with ferocity. "I love you." Her chest pitched in a sob, and it caught in his own. "I will never love another. But we deserve to share that. We do. We deserve everything. And we would give ourselves such a small portion of it. I cannot heal you. I tried to remove the thorn. The wound remains, and there's nothing I can do about it. Healing has to come from you. Please… Please understand. I have always wanted too much. My mother told me so. And that used to make me feel terrible. It's something I've been awash in these last weeks. I do want everything. It's not about being Queen, it's not about having nice dresses. It's about being loved. Don't I deserve it? Don't you deserve it."

"Livia," he said, his voice filled with torture.

"Matteo, please do not come after me for your pride."

"I do not give in," he said as she began to walk away from him.

"I know you don't."

"No. I will not be manipulated. Torture does not work on me."

"I'm not the one torturing you."

And as she took a step away from him, a sound rose in his chest that reminded him of a dying animal, guttural and filled with pain. The embodiment of everything he had ever been terrified to let out when his father had physically destroyed him.

"Do not leave me," he said.

"Can you give me what I want?"

Tears fell down her face, and he felt nothing but a blinding, stabbing pain.

"No," he said.

And then she was gone. One of his members of staff ran up to him. "Should we stop her? Shall we stop flights?"

"No," Matteo said. "No."

She was not his. And she never had been. She was *hers*. And unless he could give her even a fraction of what she was giving to him how could he…

Yes, his pride would be left in tatters by this. A second bride failing to actually follow through with the wedding, and this one in such a public way. But it didn't matter. What mattered was Livia. What an awful time to consider the feelings of another before his own for the very first time in his entire life.

But she was right.

She deserved everything. And his hands were empty.

He could offer her gowns and a castle, the world on a platter, but he did not know how to reach his own heart.

He could buy her anything she wished. He could buy himself anything he wished, for that matter, but he could not buy her. Could not make her stay.

And for the first time since he was a boy, King Matteo de la Cruz felt utterly powerless.

CHAPTER THIRTEEN

"You have become a beast."

Matteo looked up to see his brother standing in his office.

"I have always been," he growled. "This is nothing new."

"It seems remarkable to me."

"Well, I know how I feel. There is nothing different."

"Except that Livia left you devastated?"

He growled. "Do not speak her name to me."

"You are truly going to let… You're going to let your mouse leave you?"

"She wanted the one thing I cannot give, Javier. What would you have me do?"

"And that is?"

"Love."

His brother laughed, hollow and flat. "All right. And this is the part where I remember you telling me to pursue the love of Violet, all while telling me why you cannot feel it. I should, but you cannot."

"I am the King, and I can't…"

"Your bitterness is hardly helping you with your powers as a ruler, my dear brother. And I am only telling you this because it is honest. You love this woman. You do. You are trying to pretend that you don't, you are throwing every barrier in humanity in front of it. But you have loved her for the better part of nine years, and anyone around you could recognize it. But you cannot."

"No," Matteo said. "Love is…"

"A weakness? I know you think this for yourself, but what I don't understand is why. Our father had no love in his heart."

"It allows for vulnerabilities. Too many gray areas."

"You're afraid. And you had no trouble telling me that. No trouble telling me that perhaps love is worth trying since it is the one thing our father certainly never made an attempt at."

"But I loved him," Matteo said. "And he cut my skin open. I loved him, and he was a monster. I do not trust my own heart."

Love. Love was the cruelest, most dangerous thing of all. And he knew it. He *knew*.

"And here we come to it," Javier said. "You're just like me. Just the same as me. And don't give me anything about how you're the King. It makes no difference. You and I are the same. Desperately afraid of trusting our own hearts."

"But you didn't know he was a monster. I did, and still…"

"The bastard did wrong by us. There is no getting around it. No denying it. What we endured, it was not a normal childhood. He tried to destroy us. Do not let him. We never had the chance of growing up without scars. That much is true. How could we not? But we can decide what we are now. Look at Livia. Look at what she's become. From where she started… You're a king, Matteo. If she can overcome in such a way, surely you can too."

"No," Matteo said. "She is better than I am."

"And Violet is better than I am. There is a gift in loving a woman who is that strong. Who is that certain."

"I am miserable."

"So stop."

"How can it be so simple?"

"It is that simple and that difficult. You have been trained to live on an island. You have been trained to let your soul be a wasteland. To not allow for anything to touch you. For anyone. And you have decided that all emotion is a weakness. But think of how much strength it takes Livia to love you."

"It only makes me feel sorry for her."

"She did not ask for your pity. I believe she asked for your love."

"I don't know how."

"Think of your life with her. I do not know your

relationship with Livia. But I do know love. You share things. You carry each other's burdens. It is more than sex, though that is part of it. She completes you. She is your other half."

And he thought back, to these nine years that he had spent with Livia, and he knew that what his brother said was right. That it was true.

Livia was the one woman who had listened as he talked about his scars. She had seen him have nightmares and held him while he was in pain. He had taught her to dance and she had taught him to be human. She was the one he went to with all of his most pressing problems. She was the only person that he could see completing the way that he ruled the country. For she was his other half.

The one who made strength from all of his weaknesses.

His Livia.

He understood now, the manner in which she would allow him to approach. Not to claim her. But to make an offer. A real offer. For all he had done was make demands.

It was all his arrogance had allowed for.

But his love, which he realized had been there all along, hidden beneath the wall of rock… His love could humble itself. And it could ask—no, it would beg—for Livia.

"I must go."

"Of course."

"I can only hope she will still have me."

"There are some things," Javier said. "Some *people* that I believe are destined to be together. You and Livia are destined. Now you just have to go and claim it."

"I think I had better… I think I had better go and ask instead."

Livia was exhausted. She had walked around Paris all day and tried to feel something other than the crushing heartbreak that rolled through her chest in unending waves. She tried to enjoy the little magazine and art stands that were piled atop each other along the banks of the Seine. She tried to take comfort in the Arc de Triomphe and the glowing pyramid in front of the Louvre. She wandered the Musée d'Orsay aimlessly, expecting to find answers in the artwork and finding only echoes of her own sadness. She was utterly sick of herself by the time she got back to her sparsely furnished apartment. An apartment she had been surprised was still there waiting for her when she returned.

But it had been. Matteo had not taken it from her, and in fact, had bought it outright. She would have to leave, or buy it from him, or something.

But you're still hoping he'll come after you.

Yes, but not as he had done before…

You would take that. Admit it. You are weak for him…

No. She was trying to be strong for them both. Because they both deserved better than a lifetime spent beholden to the past. Than allowing Matteo's father to determine how much happiness they might have.

She took out the baguette she had brought in from the boulangerie downstairs, and simply took a bite out of the end. It was uncivilized, and she didn't care. Her apartment. Her bread.

There was a knock on the door, and her heart stilled.

Matteo did not knock.

"Yes?"

"Mouse."

It was him. She jumped up from her chair and flung the door open, and she didn't care if she had crumbs on her black top, or if she looked half so desperate as she felt. "What are you doing here?"

"I came to speak to you. I came to see you."

"Please do not tease me."

"No. This is not to tease you. Livia, I am a man in hell without you. And I have... I have turned over everything we have ever said to one another in these last years. I have thought of our life, for we have shared part of a lifetime together already. Is it not amazing?"

"It is," she said. "It is sort of amazing."

"I am flawed. Desperately so. And I did not wish to be, because I thought the only way to rule would be if I... If I somehow sanded away every vulnerability, and made myself into a cliffside. I thought I could decide to be the perfect ruler, and then I would be. But that is not to be. Livia, I told myself that a lack of emotion was needed in order to rule that way, but… You know I loved my father."

"Matteo…"

"It was so easy to say I hated him, but if it were so simple… Emotion would be black-and-white, then, would it not? I could choose good things, and turn away from the bad, but for me… It has all been one. I loved him. And he harmed me. Left me devastated. And mostly, I fear the pain that comes with this sort of feeling. I fear weakness. And I am weak standing before you."

"You are not weak," she said. "Matteo, you are the strongest man I know."

"I am weak for you. Weak now. But I would endure this weakness a thousand times over if it meant being able to have you. I would cry out in pain and think nothing of it, for I have nothing to protect if I do not have you. Nothing. I am a fool, because I had to ask my brother what love was, and what he described to me is what we are. What we had for years. It is a life shared. A burden shared."

"Matteo," she whispered. "I was very, deeply afraid to be trapped in a marriage with a man who did not love me, because I knew how easy it would be for you to abandon me. But it was my conversation with Violet that… No, you would not have left me, and I know that. But what I feared was that if I

gave you everything you wanted you would never...
You would never heal."

"You were right. You took the thorn out, and the
rest was up to me. I had to reconcile my fears, my
shortcomings. That it is not pretending I do not have
them, but rather facing them head-on, and trusting
that you, Livia, are the answer for all that I am not.
And I will do my best to be the same for you."

Her heart nearly burst. It was a beautiful thing,
this revelation. She didn't have to do all the healing,
he carried some of it all on his own. This love was
not heavy. It was a gift. Not a burden.

They did not poison one another, they gave each
other the tools to heal. To be the best they could be.

"You have been." She looked at his beloved face.
"I was such a weak, bitter creature when I arrived
here, and you gave me dreams again."

"And you have given them to me. I do not want
you to be my wife for the sake of the country. I do
not want to have children with you for the sake of
producing heirs. I want them for my sake. I want you
for the sake of my own heart. Because only then...
Only then will I be healed. But I have to ask you...
Will you marry me, Livia?"

A question. A question she could answer, and easily.

And in that question was his true change, his true
growth. Because in the question was a willingness to
be vulnerable. To admit he could not control her or

the world. He gave her a choice, and in that showed he was willing to fail.

For her.

But she wanted only to say yes. And she would.

"Yes," she said.

And he swept her up in his arms and kissed her lips. "I love you."

"I love you too, Mouse."

And Livia knew him. Knew his heart. Had for all this time.

And she knew that he meant it, from the depths of his soul. And that his love would never run out.

EPILOGUE

QUEEN LIVIA DE LA CRUZ had a title and a name now. She had spent so many years of her life without those things. Without a family name. But she had one, and a family to go with it. And now they were completing the Herculean task of taking their brood of children, along with Javier, Violet and their children, to the carnival.

Of course, being royalty, it also required that they have a security team hovering in the background, but Livia had grown used to it. And for the most part, it felt like a regular family outing. Though, none of it was regular for Matteo, Javier or herself. For they had never had family outings, and what a family was had been based on nothing other than their own dreams. Certainly not experiences.

Matteo and Livia had become the parents they *wanted* to be. Not the ones they'd had.

Therefore children were scrambling about, playing with their two cousins, creating an exceedingly well-dressed kerfuffle wherever they went.

Royalty they might be, but they were children first.

"Camila, Byron, do not scream."

Her son and daughter looked at her sheepishly. Her two younger boys looked at each other, clearly satisfied that it was not they who were on the receiving end of the scolding.

"Just one moment," Matteo said. "I'll only be a moment." Then he slipped away, and she exchanged a glance with Violet.

"What is he up to?"

"Difficult to say," Violet said, stopping for a moment and breathing heavily. She was pregnant again, and considering her and Javier's youngest child was six, she was deeply irritated with the state of things, but Livia also knew she was pleased to be adding to the family. When she wasn't angry over being pregnant again so unexpectedly.

"It's the handcuffs," she said. "I am weak for them, and I don't think."

And Livia knew exactly what she meant.

Matteo returned and he had in his hand a large serving of cotton candy.

"Matteo…" He handed it to her, and then he pulled her into an embrace, kissing her firmly on the mouth as she held tightly to the pink sweet treat.

"This is for you," he said. "Along with my promise. That for ten years I have been your husband. And I will continue to be. Forever. That's what this means now. Forever."

Tears filled her eyes, and she felt some of the remaining, lingering bruises of her past fade away.

Matteo had shown her what love was. Just how enduring it could be.

"Forever," she agreed.

And they held hands and followed their children deeper into the carnival. And Livia had never been happier.

* * * * *

Caught up in Crowning His Innocent Assistant? *Discover the thrilling first and second installments in The Kings of California trilogy:*

The Scandal Behind the Italian's Wedding
Stealing the Promised Princess

And don't forget to look out for more stories by Millie Adams!

WE HOPE YOU ENJOYED
THIS BOOK FROM

⟨H⟩ HARLEQUIN
PRESENTS

Escape to exotic locations where passion knows no bounds.

Welcome to the glamorous lives of royals and billionaires,
where passion knows no bounds. Be swept into a world
of luxury, wealth and exotic locations.

8 NEW BOOKS AVAILABLE EVERY MONTH!

HPHALO2021

#3901 BRIDE BEHIND THE DESERT VEIL

The Marchetti Dynasty

by Abby Green

After surrendering to passion with a mystery woman, Sharif Marchetti must erase their desert encounter from his memory. Until they meet again...as he lifts the veil of his convenient wife!

#3902 THE ITALIAN'S FORBIDDEN VIRGIN

Those Notorious Romanos

by Carol Marinelli

Italian tycoon Gian de Luca knows Ariana Romano is off-limits. She's his mentor's daughter, and her drama queen reputation precedes her. But when he offers her comfort one night, he's shocked to discover she's a virgin. Perhaps he's been wrong about her all along...

#3903 HIS STOLEN INNOCENT'S VOW

The Queen's Guard

by Marcella Bell

For billionaire Drake Andros, only marriage and an heir from Helene d'Tierrza will recover what was stolen from him. Their chemistry may persuade her to help him, but her vow of innocence may complicate his plan...

#3904 ONE HOT NEW YORK NIGHT

Wanted: A Billionaire

by Melanie Milburne

A sizzling night of passion is exactly what Zoey Brackenfield needs. And since it's with Finn O'Connell, business rival and notorious playboy, there's zero chance of heartbreak. That is, until she starts craving his exhilarating touch...

YOU CAN FIND MORE INFORMATION ON UPCOMING HARLEQUIN TITLES, FREE EXCERPTS AND MORE AT HARLEQUIN.COM.

HPCNMRB0321

Love Harlequin romance?

DISCOVER.

Be the first to find out about promotions, news and exclusive content!

Facebook.com/HarlequinBooks

Twitter.com/HarlequinBooks

Instagram.com/HarlequinBooks

Pinterest.com/HarlequinBooks

YouTube.com/HarlequinBooks

ReaderService.com

EXPLORE.

Sign up for the Harlequin e-newsletter and download a free book from any series at **TryHarlequin.com**

CONNECT.

Join our Harlequin community to share your thoughts and connect with other romance readers!
Facebook.com/groups/HarlequinConnection

HSOCIAL2021